For Christine
in honor of our
Shared community +
our shared love of
the word !

Wendy Belcher
7/6/88

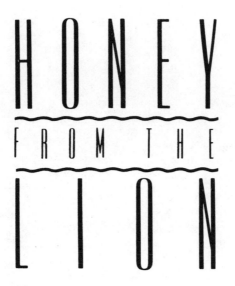

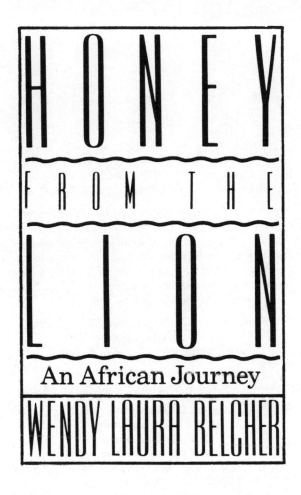

HONEY FROM THE LION

An African Journey

WENDY LAURA BELCHER

E. P. DUTTON NEW YORK

Published in the United States by E. P. Dutton,
a division of NAL Penguin Inc.,
2 Park Avenue, New York, N.Y. 10016.

Published simultaneously in Canada by
Fitzhenry and Whiteside, Limited, Toronto.

Library of Congress Cataloging-in-Publication Data
Belcher, Wendy Laura.
Honey from the lion.
1. Ghana—Social life and customs. 2. Ghana—
Religious life and customs. 3. Belcher, Wendy Laura—
Journeys—Ghana. I. Title.
DT510.4.B38   1987   966.7'05   87-24443

ISBN: 0-525-24596-0

W

Designed by Steven N. Stathakis

1 3 5 7 9 10 8 6 4 2

First Edition

For Mary

How can a person be born when she is old?
Can a person enter a second time
into her mother's womb and be born?

—JOHN 3:4

TABLE OF TIDES

AUTHOR'S NOTE

This book relates some of the experiences I had while spending nine months of 1982–83 in Ghana, West Africa. I had lived in Africa before then—as a child. My father's work as a medical doctor took us to Goandar, Ethiopia, from 1966 to 1969 and to Accra, Ghana, from 1970 to 1976. In both places, he taught medicine and researched rural health. When I was twenty-one, I returned to Ghana to work for a national linguistic group run by Ghanaians. Their interests lay in literacy work and bible translation in mother tongues. I worked as a writer and a photographer for them, traveling to the villages where translators worked and developing publicity materials. The majority of that year I lived in the town of Tamale, over four hundred miles north of the coast.

The views and events of this book reflect my experiences in Ghana and should not be construed as a comprehensive report on Ghana's people, politics, or economy. The names of the Ghanaians have been changed to protect their privacy.

ACKNOWLEDGMENTS

Many Ghanaians to whom I am deeply indebted I cannot thank by name. I can only hope that this book will show some measure of the love I bear for you.

Thanks to John Lemly for his guidance in this book's early stages, to Richard A. Johnson and other members of the Mount Holyoke College English Department for their encouragement, to Patricia Lorange Taylor for her edit of the first draft, and to Carole DeSanti for always seeing what this book could be. Thanks also to my early readers for their criticism: Kwaku and Lisa Mensah, Bonnie Berry, Sharon Martin, Gayle Boss, Naomi Thiers, Paula Diehl, Newman Fair, and Joanna Phinney, not to mention those who figured in the book whose comments were most helpful.

Thanks to those who slipped me money: Kirsty M. Haining, Ellen Renzetti, Gayle Boss, Ingrid Karen Young, Nancy Estler, Dixcy Bosley, Gloria Gomez, and in particular my parents, Donald and Sheila Belcher, without whom—nothing.

I would not have written this book if it weren't for Maddy Hewitt, who first found my story interesting, and Robert S. Keene, whose death forced me to seize life.

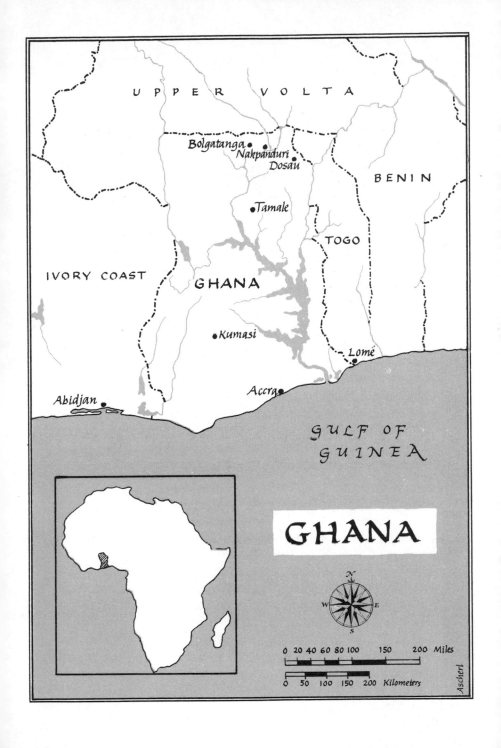

UPPER VOLTA

Bolgatanga
Nakpanduri
Dosau

BENIN

Tamale

TOGO

IVORY COAST

GHANA

Kumasi

Lomé

Abidjan

Accra

GULF OF
GUINEA

GHANA

0 20 40 60 80 100   150   200 Miles

0   50   100   150   200 Kilometers

Ascherl

ADVENT

The Coming To

A wave of wet heat swept over me. It pushed by, pungent with asphalt and ocean and greenness. I swayed and clutched the metal railing. Its coolness did nothing to mute this sensation: the warm air was amniotic fluid, and in it I was moving back into something both forgotten and deeply known.

Looking up as I descended the steps, I could see the terminal across the shimmering airstrip. Ghana's Kotoka International Airport, once crisp and Western, now seemed as much a part of the landscape as a baobab tree. A young soldier surveyed us from the army tank lumbering past. The disembarking passengers ahead bore tins of vegetable oil and packages of sugar. Sweat sprung to my skin.

Inside seemed cool after the piercing sunlight, but that feeling soon evaporated. I stood in a chalk white corridor with high ceilings. Wooden desks punctuated its length. The portly Ghanaian in front of me frowned at the immigration officials, flipped his documents open, and was waved through. I was less sure. The documents I had to sign were detailed and long. The official glanced with

3

disinterest at my signature and nodded me on to the next formality.

I shifted my bag to the other shoulder and brushed a moth from my shirt. Starting for the next desk, I gazed around me. Nothing must escape my notice or memory. A journey always starts with a sign, I knew. Something to prepare me for what would follow. The trick was to identify it.

One summer I had worked in Alaska slinging salmon. We traveled from Seattle to Bristol Bay by ship, taking the famed Inside Passage. We passed mountains ravaged like Mars, trawlers plumbing the green depths, and glaciers slowly sliding into the sea.

As I was standing on the deck one day, mesmerized by the eternal wave the bow of the ship carved, a fellow worker pointed out a line of debris floating on the surface. It stretched away as far as I could see. The water where the debris floated was flat and shiny like a scar. Two currents met there, he explained, and negated each other, creating between them static water, which trapped flotsam. The flotsam could not escape the deadening space between the conflicting currents.

I was the same. As an American raised in Africa, I drifted at the meeting of two cultures, the African and the Western. I was caught between them, belonging to neither. I hoped by my return to this African country to free myself.

At the airport, people pressed round the next desk. Large women in traditional cloths were wedged sideways between slim men in suits. The man checking passports had set his face into angry indifference and was plucking documents from among those shoved forward. He never spoke or looked up. The meek may inherit the earth, a Ghanaian had once said to me, but the aggressive will run it until then. I stepped closer to push my passport forward.

After it was checked, I entered the pandemonium of

4

the baggage claim room and hesitated. Mountains of baggage overwhelmed the defunct conveyor belts. Suitcases were few, bags and boxes in abundance, all bulging and cinched with string. People packed the room, greeting family members and cheering finds made among the unmarked luggage. Soldiers wearing khaki uniforms and machine guns lounged everywhere. One sprawled flat on his belly, his feet and hands dangling from the counter he slept on, his face jammed against the barrel of his gun.

A tall, thin man appeared in front of me, his face the even black of the tropical African.

"Peace Corps?" he shouted, leaning forward, trying to make himself heard above the din.

"Uh, no," I shouted back. "I'm with the Institute of—"

He interrupted my attempt to get out the whole name of the institute by signaling to some men across the room and yelling, "Peace Corps!" My protests that I was not in the Peace Corps went unheard. Perhaps the Peace Corps was the only organization he knew of that didn't send someone for white women traveling alone.

Several more men arrived then, and the one who found me gave a charming smile. "Madam!" he proclaimed. "I am Kofi. We help you. Come this way and we fetch your things."

This was the welcome I had expected. How wonderful it was, I thought, to be back in a country where people freely offered hospitality to a stranger.

When they discovered my suitcase at the bottom of one heap, I grinned at them. Kofi swept me through the lines at customs by declaring, "Peace Corps! Peace Corps!" whenever the officials tried to open my suitcase. The officials seemed unimpressed but nevertheless waved me on.

My newfound friends carried my suitcase and bag to a taxi. Rows of palm trees, one of which shaded us, alternated with rows of parking spaces. Above us spread a hazy sky, and above the pavement lay its inversion—heat mirages. The road stretched away like the mirror of a smooth sea.

The men watched me expectantly. As I realized what they waited for, I felt first betrayed and then foolish. How could I have believed they would expect nothing in return? I wiped the sweat from my face with the side of my shirt and remembered that I had no Ghanaian currency.

"I'm so sorry," I said, squinting, "but I don't have any cedis to give you."

Kofi was not dismayed. He eyed my pale skin, blue eyes, and thin blond hair. "Madam, we no want cedis. You get dollars?"

"Well, yes, I have a few." I unfolded the eight dollars I had left and handed them over uncertainly.

He took these while shaking his head. "Madam. This no be enough. We all of us help you."

"I have no more, except for traveler's checks."

He smiled. "Oh, we take that."

"But only a business can take them."

"Oh, no, madam. We can take them. Don't worry."

Suddenly I came to myself. It was illegal to give out foreign currency, and that law was strictly enforced. Eight dollars was a larger tip than I usually gave; five people unnecessary for handling one suitcase. I reverted to the pidgin English I would have used as a child in Africa. "You abuse me! No more dash."

The men left with pained expressions. I discovered later that at the *kalabule,* or black market, rate those eight dollars were worth about two months' salary. "It is bad, it is bad," says the buyer, but when he goes away, he boasts.

As I watched them walk away, I felt paralyzed. I knew Africa well enough to be embarrassed. Not only had I—who should have known better—helped them trick me but I was so wealthy here they asked for more than the fortune I had just given. And yet I was enough of a

Westerner to be angry, too. What I would have gladly given them, I begrudged being taken from me.

The return of my childhood heartmates, shame and anger, was not the homecoming I had looked for. I had forgotten how strong the riptide could be. Like a person coming up for the last time, I sucked in air. Lord, is this my sign? And as I turned toward the taxi, the wet African air engulfed me.

The taxi driver lifted my suitcase into the backseat of his Toyota. I eased myself in on the other side. Because the seat lacked its plastic cover, I sat on foam. Between my feet I saw pavement. My window had no glass; the opposite side had no door at all. I decided to concentrate on the scenery.

Beyond the cars and palm trees, green hills undulated. The soil's red color bloomed through the lush vegetation. Now, during the wet season, the earth translated into leaf.

After securing my door, the driver walked around the front of the car. He was middle-aged. Tribal scars plowed both cheeks; the refining of his natural state showed his cultivation. He wore a long, loose shirt and thick-strapped sandals. The lettering on his bumper said BY THE BLOOD OF JESUS, and from his mirror hung a pink plastic rosary.

The rosary reminded me. Only twelve hours earlier I had been viewing the dizzying splendors of the Vatican. Caravaggio's warm figures rising out of darkness, Michelangelo's muscular, mythic beings, Rodin's Paul reeling before the light. Rich colors, gold leaf, encrusted jewels, marble sleek as skin. The contrast with the dilapidated airport and taxi was disturbing, as if I had been smothered with perfume and then required to smell salt.

"Madam, you are going where?" the taxi driver asked, examining me over his shoulder.

I gave him the full name of the institute.

He frowned, puzzled. "I don't know this place."

I couldn't locate my map in my bag, but I remembered the general area. "I think it's in Labadi Estate."

"Okay." America's language is its widest ranging export. The driver grinned, reaching for the ignition. "We go there. By chance, we find it." I grinned back. The car shuddered to life, and we lurched off.

Exiting the parking lot, we swung past the statue of Kotoka, a general who had died while helping to overthrow Ghana's first government. Kotoka had run for his life from the heart of the city to this site. The statue rose from where he had been shot. He stood in a dignified pose, wearing formal clothing, and showed no trace of his desperate race for liberty.

We turned toward Accra, Ghana's capital, passing a billboard bearing the portrait of the head of state, Jerry Rawlings, and a quote from him in English. The portrait showed a young, handsome man in military uniform without regalia. His light skin spoke of mixed Western and African heritages. The quote stated Ghana's need to help herself before she could depend on the help of other countries and was placed where every arriving foreigner, or returning Ghanaian, could see it.

The city of Accra lies like an open fan along the coast. The handle of the fan is the oldest part of the city—a seventeenth-century Danish slave castle overlooking the ocean—and the outside of the fan is the most recent. In concentric half circles around the castle are the buildings of successive eras: first the British government buildings, then Kwame Nkrumah's monuments, next the embassies of postindependence, and beyond the sprawl of the modern city. Most of the country stretches north of Accra, rather than to the east or west. Only the more populated southern part of Ghana is tropical rain forest; the majority of the country is scrub-covered plains. Accra itself lies on a coastal plain.

As we drove west into the outskirts of Accra, I noticed that the city had deteriorated in the six years since I had lived there. People had told me I would find it much changed. But I was struck more by the old, familiar things that I had so long associated with home. Women selling shaved oranges. Red and brown lizards doing push-ups on the pavement. A wooden stall lined with vegetables. Babies strapped on women's backs. A man riding a bicycle with a mattress balanced on his head. Rusty cars shooting by, their horns more reliable than their brakes. Mamie wagons—trucks adapted for public transport—with painted slogans such as GOD'S TIME IS THE BEST, PRINCE OF PEACE, and WHO KNOWS?

We drove past the Continental Hotel, where my family used to have our hair cut, and the military hospital near our former home. Down that road a friend had lived, I remembered, and up that one there the highlife band could be heard for miles on a Saturday night. The traffic circles, called roundabouts, had different names now. Their names changed with each new government, but people were always at least one government behind in the name they used. At a stop sign, the sweet smell of roasting plantain rose from a vendor's fire, and a man bent to swing his machete against the roadside grass. My excitement, momentarily pierced at the airport, inflated again.

"It's so wonderful to be back in Ghana!"

"You lived here before this time?" the taxi driver asked, glancing at me.

"Oh yes. With my family when I was a girl. On Switchback Road." My first memories are of Africa, and I didn't leave Africa "for good" until I was well on my way into adolescence.

"Eh!" The driver clucked his tongue. "In those days Ghana be fine *pa*. You go to Kingsway and buy nice shoes. Nobody like for make palaver. Now, everything is *nyama-nyama*." He shrugged expressively. "As for this my country . . ."

9

"Things are hard?"

"In fact! It hard pass. You see this car. I no fit buy parts. I never think I see days like these."

Imports were at a minimum, I had heard before I came. Seventy percent of the nonoperative vehicles in Ghana simply needed tires. Gasoline was rationed, and a driver could wait in gas lines for days. Department stores had closed for lack of goods. Beauty salons, auto shops, and photo labs performed their services only for those who could provide supplies.

"Why is this?"

"Madam?"

"Why are things so hard?"

"I don't know." He was silent for a moment, negotiating the space between an articulated truck turning left and the deep ditch running along the road edge. "They say the leaders have stolen from the people."

"This new man—Rawlings—he has said that?"

"Yoh. J.J. say bad men have ruled Ghana to steal from her. True, true. Anyhow, some may not believe, but since the time when your people left we get plenty trouble. In my hometown, my father he be asking me, 'The queen come when?' "

"You're joking!"

"No!" he exclaimed, offended. "What! When *oburoni* here we no get these killings. These young boys! They refuse the advice of old men. What can you expect?"

This was not what I wanted to hear. "I didn't think you would ever want the British back."

"I be coming from the North. As for my people, we never want the British to go. The Ashantis trouble us too much. We no be like them. They will never let a man from the North rule. I tell you." He nodded.

"These are hard things you are saying."

"Well, they be hard times. Except for God we never live."

I studied the back of his head. Had he told me about

10

the good old days to gain my approval, and a tip? Or was it prejudiced of me to suspect his sincerity? I sighed and turned back to the window. Ask no questions, and you'll be told no lies.

We reached the Labadi Estate, a part of Accra that borders the waters of the Gulf of Guinea. Although I could not see the ocean, it was pervasive: its muted pound the city's heartbeat, its salty wind the city's breath. The ocean spoke to me as the voice of an earlier time.

When I was ten, the boy across the street drowned. I had not known Michael well, but his absence loomed as he had not. The undertow at the beach was strong, and he had been pulled out to sea when no one was looking. Fishermen found his body washed up on the shore three days later. Felix, the taxi driver who took us to school each morning, told me that bodies often washed up after several days.

At night, in my bed, I imagined Michael struggling against the current—the water in his mouth, the leaden weight of his limbs, the terrifying bottomlessness. If he could have struggled for three days, I wondered, would he have been brought back safely to the shore? Could anyone struggle that long? Perhaps he had quit too soon. How did a person know when to give up and when to keep going?

Felix told us Michael's mother had been cursed. She was Ghanaian and her devoted husband, Swiss. The boy was beautiful. Even I, so young, could see it: his parents' races merged in a golden gracefulness. Felix said that a woman who was jealous of the mother's fine house, faithful husband, and beautiful son had cursed her.

"I know about these things, curses," Felix declared to my brother and me, wide-eyed in the backseat. He wrenched the wheel to dodge a boy selling *The Daily Graphic*. "Some be jealous of this my taxi. But as for me, they can't harm me. I am a Christian." He slapped his

11

chest with his palm. "Jesus will cause their curses to bounce from me."

For three months afterward, when my father asked if we should visit the beach that week, I shook my head. Then, one week, he did not ask. We simply went. I sat on the dry sand and watched the ocean suck up the land and vomit it back. I did not swim.

The next week I walked down to the edge. The ocean was green and deep and slow. I waded in. How odd, I thought. The ocean reeked so little of death. The water was warm and the sun bright. The treacherous current tugged gently at my legs, licking the sand away from my toes. I had wanted death to be something concrete. There, I could say. From a distance. That's where death lives. I waded out a little farther and crouched—chest forward, face up—as a wave broke full over me.

"Madam." The taxi driver's voice reeled me back. We were pulling into a street with potholes the size of bathtubs. I thought we would have to retreat—their placement seemed malicious—but the driver navigated them with easy disdain. "Where be this place?" he asked.

I had no idea, so we circled the area trying to spy a sign. I had been expecting offices, but on either side of the street stood simple bungalow residences. We found ourselves at a dead end, and as the driver reversed his way out, I glanced back. Behind us rose a faded billboard. A full-faced man saluted us with a bottle of Star beer. His lips were parted, as if he was about to speak, and I heard in my mind another voice.

When I was still ten, a black visitor with a British accent had attended one of the dinner parties my parents often gave. A heavy, elegantly dressed man, he moved carefully. Round glasses rested on his nose, and a mustache etched his full mouth.

He dominated the dinner conversation, his interests so broad they overshadowed even my mother's. I listened, enthralled, my curried chicken forgotten. Our dining room became the world I dreamed of when he spoke about the latest shows in London and delivered an occasional apropos comment in Latin. His language translated me beyond our simple furniture and the insects batting at the screens.

For I did not love Ghana as I had loved Ethiopia—where we'd lived until I was seven. Ghana lacked magic, a quality I had come to expect of Africa in Ethiopia.

In the late 1960s, the highlands of Ethiopia where we had lived had been green and cool. Every afternoon, rain refreshed the land. Sharp mountains ringed the plateau our town rested on. Life was medieval in everything but name. Illuminated manuscripts, icons, and moat-encircled castles were in daily use around me. Unmuzzled oxen threshed the grain. A descendant of King David sat on the throne. Vessels of papyrus plied Lake Tana, gliding between the islands of silent monasteries. During the celebration of Meskal, a two-story cross was covered with tiny yellow flowers and set alight. My brother and I leaned from our bedroom window, straining with the men who raced round until the perfumed tongue of fire listed and fell.

What in this flat, brown land of West Africa could rival that? Only after the rains, when the same fecund smell rose from the land, did Ghana and Ethiopia seem similar to me. Now, listening to our visitor, I imagined other places might be the Eden that Ethiopia had been for me.

It was during dessert that I realized. I don't remember how, but it dawned on me that there was something decidedly Ghanaian about the visitor's drawled speech and extended stories. Yes, I thought slowly, the man was not British but Ghanaian. And with this realization, coming so quickly I could not avoid the mud it spattered, I suddenly found his conversation pompous and tiresome.

I blushed and, embarrassed by my naked face, looked

down at my bowl of fruit. I was horrified; the manner I thought gracious in a Briton I considered officious in a Ghanaian. I knew then that whatever had made Ethiopia an Eden, whatever Ghana lacked, I lacked, too.

No longer expecting enchantment from Ghana, I began to see. At the beach, a fisherman's canoe took us plunging into the bright surf and out to an island where I found a monkey's skull. Going inland, we drove up into the cool hills of the Aburi Botanical Gardens, where I first saw a chameleon alter its brilliant green for the brown safety of a tree trunk. On the coast, we descended from the white terraces of windswept castles to the dank, silent rooms of human traffic. If Ethiopia had been my nurse, Ghana was my teacher.

Abruptly, the taxi was out of reverse, and I turned as we jerked forward. At the next intersection, the driver stopped. I looked at him, puzzled, for I didn't see any sign.

He pointed at the house we had halted by. "Make we ask here where for this place be. He be pastor."

"Do you live around here?"

"No, madam. I live the other side."

"How do you know who lives here?"

He did not understand the question, and I thought better of repeating it. The network of people any one Ghanaian knew was complex because of the size of families and the bonds of tribe.

I trailed him through the iron gate and up the short concrete path. The house was whitewashed and curtained. A small girl answered the door. She greeted us with her eyes averted. "You are welcome."

Inside we sat on a couch covered with orange market cloth. The furniture was smooth and wooden, the floor cool tile. Across from us opened louvered windows, beyond which I caught a glimpse of the sand-moored ocean. Chickens squawked outside and a coconut tree rustled in

14

the ocean breeze, sounding like the turning of pages in church. Smoke rose from a charcoal cooking fire.

The girl left us to wait for ten minutes. The taxi driver shifted restlessly, but did not touch *The People's Graphic* that lay open to the obituaries. I wondered what we were interrupting. Then three women of varying ages entered. I smiled my most winning smile, but the three did not break their silence. I took my cue from the taxi driver and remained silent, too.

While we waited another ten minutes, I examined the women's faces, furtively at first, and then openly, since they did not glance back. I could not describe their faces in terms of lines, as I could Caucasian faces. A line is the shortest distance between two points. These faces did not trade in such abbreviations. Their approach was roundabout, each curve moving into the next, any one leading to any other. No beginning and no end, everything linked.

The older woman turned and gave me a steadfast gaze. Uneasy, I glanced away and then back. Was her face mute witness to our distance or just deceptively different? Suddenly I was wearier than I remembered being. I leaned forward and pressed my fists to my ears. Enough, I thought. This is all coming back too quickly. I had forgotten the unending questions, the debilitating uncertainty. How had I ever managed? My fists quieted the sounds from outside, but I found no refuge. Under my hands my blood thundered through its mysterious miles. Even my own body was a foreign land.

When the pastor arrived, I made the effort to straighten. After lowering himself into a chair, he became still as the air at noon. Sweat slid down his temples and beaded under his eyes.

"You are welcome."

"We thank you," said the taxi driver, shifting to the edge of his seat. "How do you find the day?"

15

"It is well." Then, unexpectedly circumventing the courtesies, "Can I help you?"

The driver, appearing glad of this haste, told the pastor what we were seeking.

"As for that place, I don't know," the pastor said with a frown. "I'm thinking you will go by that side." He pointed.

After a silence, one of the women spoke to him in a local language, pointing in another direction. There followed a discussion in the same language, which I did not understand. The words of the conversation, relieved of their semantic freight, rushed by me faster than they would have in English. From their pointing, I gathered they had agreed on the direction opposite to the pastor's original one. The taxi driver nodded his head and stood.

"We thank you," he repeated. "We go now."

I smiled and nodded at them, and the women responded in kind. The pastor remained still. Diffident, I faltered forward, drew back, then pitched ahead to shake his hand. His gaze told no stories. The taxi driver turned and took the lead by striding to the car.

We had actually been quite close to the institute. Just a minute later, we pulled up to it. The institute's lengthy title scarcely fit the small place. Surrounded by a concrete wall with heavy gates were two bungalows, a small patch of grass, and a garden.

What surprised me most of all, however, was the stench of alcohol. Despite the ocean lying just a field away, the smell of fermentation was overpowering.

A large white woman in a sleeveless dress emerged, arranged to pay the taxi driver what she exclaimed was an exorbitant amount, and led me into the yard. She was the first Westerner I had seen that day.

The woman's name was Madeleine, and she was the hostess/manager for the resthouse, or small traveler's lodge, the institute ran. One of the bungalows in the compound was the resthouse, and the other was her family's.

"You made it from the airport by yourself?" she asked with surprise, in an accent I later learned was Swiss. She and her husband had been told I was arriving on the evening flight and had been planning to meet me then.

"Well," I explained with embarrassment, "I had a map, but somehow I mislaid it and then I got some help at the airport that I could have done without, but, well"—I shrugged and smiled—"here I am."

Madeleine laughed and said approvingly, "You have been in Ghana before."

I nodded. "I knew I'd get here eventually." Now that I could see that the institute, which had sounded so formal, was just a house in a city of nearly a million people, my confidence about finding it seemed misplaced.

I surveyed the yard. Five barefoot children hung out of a guava tree, staring. Their hair—blond to black, straight to curly—spoke of different nationalities, but their bodies were universally brown with dirt. Ten years ago I would have been one of them. I smiled, but they didn't smile back. Neither would I have. I glanced away and then saw what created the fetid smell: a brown mass of crushed sugarcane spread on burlap sacking.

Madeleine answered my unspoken question. "It's the mash used to make *pito*," a brew like beer. I wondered from the amount of mash if they were keeping the city in drink.

"Daniel, my husband, buys it from the brewer to feed to our rabbits. We grow rabbits for meat since there is no meat in the markets. It's drying now; then we can feed it to them."

"How long does it take to dry?" I asked, looking at the mash spread beneath a window of the resthouse and wondering which room I had.

"A week, maybe two," Madeleine divulged with an inscrutable look. I nodded sagely, as if this situation was fine with me, and she gave a huge laugh. I was hoping she would tell me she had been teasing, but such was not

17

the case. She just put her arm around me, as if I had passed a test, and led me into her house.

Two weeks later—the day before I was to leave Accra for the institute's office in Tamale—I went to the airport with Madeleine's husband, Daniel, and his assistant, a Ghanaian named Alfonze. We were to pick up some travelers.

My newly attuned eyes saw that the airport contained an abundance of things not found elsewhere in the country. The lobby itself reflected the country's decrepit state—plastic signs swung loose, counters were battered and scuffed, the lights looked like they had been shot out—but the Ghanaian travelers brought to mind the extravagance of Marie Antoinette. In the heavy heat, I noticed a woman with a white fur coat slung over one arm, stiletto heels, huge tinted glasses, and bruise-colored lipstick. A man swaggered by in a crisp orange cloth splashed with red. From his neatly picked hair to his shiny sandals, he was the image of the new African, merging the traditional and the modern. He looked through us with studied nonchalance.

Daniel asked if the plane was on time, and the clerk shrugged. Africa yields to no agenda. Alfonze leaned toward me and whispered with mock severity, "Wait and see."

"It will come when it comes," I whispered back. In two weeks Alfonze had taught me much about the language of bureaucracy.

Suddenly I noticed a swift but silent swirl of movement on the far side of the lobby. Nothing distinct—just the motion and a slim arm shooting out. A noiseless wave rippled through the crowd and toward the door. A soldier behind the counter hiked his gun up, leapt onto the counter, and flung himself into the throng.

"Thief!" someone shouted.

The place erupted. People ran outside, shouting. The high-ceilinged lobby drained, and we stood alone by the

18

counters like ghosts in an abandoned ballroom. I could not see what was happening.

Just when we thought the thief must have escaped, three soldiers returned dragging the man in orange I had just seen. The raucous crowd ebbed around him. The man hid his hands in his tunic but walked as if no soldiers surrounded him, as if capture had freed him. His head was raised, and I could see him looking others in the eye, seeking contact in the decaying splendor of the Kotoka International Airport.

Some confusion arose then about who owned the wallet he had tried to take. The soldiers finally pushed the two claimants and the thief into a room and followed them, one soldier slamming the door shut after a last fierce look at the crowd.

The woman with the fur coat spun on her slim heels and exited. Through the hiatus she left in the crowd I caught a glimpse of the statue of somber, martyred Kotoka. Then the crowd flowed in a wave across my view.

EPIPHANY

The Visit

Beyond the frame of my car window, flat land stretched. A cloud had not marred the even gray of the sky in months. The sky's lack of character did not prevent it from dominating the scene, however. Harmattan dust hung in the air like a mosquito net, translating the once solid forms a mile away into blurred parodies of themselves. Day after day the black-red dust sifted down, as if some great battle brawled in the heavens and the dried blood of the contestants was being strewn like incense before the winds.

Blackened grass patched the parched ground. The grass-burning season had taken its toll even here, where no one farmed. Just twelve stunted trees littered the dead land.

It was January. The rains would not come for several months. When they did come, the thick growth would obscure everything beyond the edge of the road. But for now, the sweep of the land lay bared. I could almost smell the desert lurking, waiting to reclaim the land it had lost to rudimentary vegetation.

The road was built up like a small dike. When Mary

stopped the pickup truck briefly, I walked down the bank and out into the silent expanse. The sunlight beat about my shoulders and head like wings. In my mouth and nostrils, I could feel the gritty dust. The long-completed process of decay had sanitized the dust to tastelessness.

The wind rattled through the dry branches of the tree nearby. I closed my eyes. I tried to imagine the wind gusting off the ocean and the slap of rigging. But I could not get past the heat and dust and silence.

I opened my eyes. Seeing anew the scorched land, I spotted a bright yellow blur. I walked toward it, wondering how a bit of plastic came to be there. Amid the ashes and the dust nestled a flower. Veined, dewy, untouched by dust. When I raised my head again, I could see many pinpoints of canary yellow. Look and you will find. I walked back to the car, leaping over the cracks in the soil. Puffs of dust rose to mark my passing. As the pickup started moving, I glanced over my shoulder and could still see that harbinger of renewal.

I had been back in Ghana, living in Tamale, for about three months by then. Tamale was a town on a plain far north of the border of green that edged the coast where I had lived before. The land was dry, and its people angular. It lay midway between the Sahara and the Atlantic, and so had become the crossroads for several trading routes. As the capital of the Northern Region, Tamale was graced with a fine secondary school, a radio station, and a modern hospital. Both water and electricity systems existed. The roads going to the points of the compass were paved.

Despite these amenities, however, Tamale was something of an outpost. Boys, lean and alert as their loping dogs, herded cattle through the streets. One of the town's two gas stations lifted its broken neon sign outside the chief's thatched palace. Three machine guns rose from the lawn in front of the police station. Men prayed in mosques that were stones arranged in the outline of a building, and women kept their heads covered.

After three months of being confined to Tamale, I was glad to be traveling. As I rested an arm on the window, delighted with the way the land rushed by, I realized how much I had missed the freedom of driving.

We whipped past women trudging with headloads of firewood steadied on coiled cloths. Each wore a Western blouse and an African cloth wrapped around her waist. They stopped to lift their scarves over their faces to prevent the dust from choking them. I turned to look, but could not tell whether I saw longing or disgust in their eyes.

I glanced at Mary, my companion. Ever since her youth she had worked in northern Ghana, so perhaps it is irrelevant to state that Mary was Irish. Her accent had been eroded by a lifetime among the wash of foreign tongues. The barren landscape framed by her window in turn framed her weathered profile. Her scarf was tied carefully about her hair. She pursed her thin upper lip and full lower lip over her protruding teeth. Her short eyelashes barely shaded her hazel eyes, their yellow-brown matching the dusty earth. She drove well, both hands grasping the steering wheel, her back not touching the seat.

The first time I had seen Mary, she had been singing hymns with the others during the morning break at the institute. I had been in Tamale a month by then, during which time she had been in her village translating. When I entered, she was sitting straight, with her feet and knees pressed together in a pose that struck me as more girlish than prim. She wore wire-framed glasses and tilted her head to look at the songbook she held at a distance. The posture might have appeared haughty, but on her it was curiously touching, a sign of infirmity.

These two impressions startled me. From what I had heard about her around the institute, Mary was neither

25

girlish nor infirm. I was disappointed: surely a woman of her character would bear some physical sign of it.

Mary was one of those single women who leave home and family to follow a religious calling to a foreign place. Such women, coming most often from conservative religious traditions, would never call themselves feminists. Yet, they leave behind everything their culture says is important to women to do things in another place that they would not be allowed to do at home. They are paradoxical women: parochial but adventurous, lovers of children and yet childless, domestic at heart and yet dedicated to unworldly work.

In the year that I was born, 1962, Mary had arrived in Ghana, after a three-week sail, with one suitcase and a barrel of belongings. She transferred by canoe to the palm-fringed shore, her unlashed barrel swaying dangerously. Mary perched behind those few belongings, the only bulwark between her and complete change, and with unspoken emotion watched as the mass of the waiting crowd—her future—became individual bodies, and then faces, and then watchful eyes.

Twenty years later, Mary had finished one translation of the New Testament and was halfway through another. She had painstakingly proofread and retyped the same texts dozens of times. She had wrestled with grammar and syntax and spelling and meaning in the ancient attempt to create from words the life-giving force. She had accomplished these tasks despite having seven different partners, eight homes, and many illnesses. Most of the time, she had been alone and on the move. But she had continued to work in order that the logos might be spoken and thereby become flesh, to make the word conversions that would make human converts.

Given these facts, I expected a woman of large proportions and larger movements. Mary, however, was slim and remote. Her posture was perfect, her long fingers those of a pianist. She could have been regal, but she restrained her stride just short of a glide, and the enforced utilitarian movement made her look awkward. Her clothes always had flair, despite their outmoded ankle length, and fit her tall frame well.

Her reserve, the neatness of her clothing, and her quiet voice formed my lasting image of her. And yet, this demureness was broken by her odd walk, weak teeth, and rare smile. Rare not because it was infrequent but because it was a rare kind of smile to have—an unmixed gladness in the present, which shot unexpectedly across her plain face.

I suppose it is not surprising then that I became fascinated by Mary. She had a reticence that inspired inquiry and a courage I wanted. She had succeeded in the kind of heroism I aimed for in my own life. A woman who worked with words, alone and in a foreign land. Surely she had overcome the deadening space between cultures. I could learn from her. I began to look for the opportunity to watch her closely.

And so I found myself traveling with Mary across this wasteland. I had brought my notebook and intended to get to the bottom of her life in the course of my three-day visit. With this information I also intended to write an article for the institute's newsletter. During our trip to Dosau, the village where Mary worked, I started to ask her some of the questions I had prepared. "How did you get into translation work? What was your childhood like? What are the disadvantages and advantages of the work?"

Mary spoke awkwardly. She told me later that because of the years spent translating she often stumbled when phrasing things. "Every time I think of something in English, I switch it around so that it is ready to be translated."

Mary had been born and raised with many brothers and sisters on a large farm in Northern Ireland. "I was

27

used to being alone, more than most perhaps, because we lived in a rural area. A farm girl spends most of her time alone, outside. But whenever I wanted to be with someone I could be with my family. I had a very happy, secure childhood. It's a good background to have if you are often alone."

Ever since she had been a young girl she had wanted to be a missionary, although her conception of a missionary had been limited. "When I was young, I thought being a missionary was standing under a shady tree and preaching," she said. "I haven't done that at all." She read the biographies of David Livingstone and Mary Slessor avidly. "I suppose that's why I was always so interested in Africa."

At fifteen years old, riding her bicycle to church, Mary reached the top of a rise that overlooked her small town and heard God call her to be a missionary nurse.

I interrupted. "Just like that? You were just riding a bike and you heard God?"

"Yes."

"What did it feel like? What exactly did you hear?"

"It wasn't spectacular. I just heard him."

"You weren't scared?"

"Not then."

I felt a flash of irritation. I hoped that she would describe other things in more exciting terms. This was hardly the stuff of heroism, or even journalism. I did not think to ask the question "When?"

Mary continued after a pause. She followed the call and went into training as a nurse. In her early twenties, she went to Labrador, Canada, for a year and then to South Africa. In South Africa she worked in a hospital for Africans near where a German missionary had translated the New Testament into the local language. There Mary learned how much it meant to a people to have the bible in their own language.

As she thought about her work, she came to believe

28

that it was more important to help people find eternal life than to help them lead a healthy present life. "No matter how much a nurse knows about how to heal, there comes a time when a person cannot be helped by her skill. People have to die eventually. It is better to prepare someone for that."

Mary went back to England and attended bible college, where she heard about Wycliffe Bible Translators. This organization seemed an answer to her prayers. After joining Wycliffe, Mary went to Ghana, the first African country Wycliffe entered, arriving just six months after the work began.

At this point in her story, we made a detour to stop at Nakpanduri, a village on an escarpment overlooking the plains. Kwame Nkrumah, the man who led Ghana into independence and became the country's first president, had built a resthouse for himself on the edge of the escarpment because of its view. We threaded our way through the slabs of slate and twisted scrub trees before reaching the edge. The harmattan dust prevented us from seeing the plain. Even the trees just below us emerged from the haze as only a few strokes.

We returned to the car and were about to leave when a stranger, a Ghanaian in his thirties, came up and introduced himself as Godfrey. He wore leather shoes and pressed trousers with a matching shirt. Probably no person within five hundred miles of him was dressed so. He invited us into the resthouse.

On entering I was stunned to see things I hadn't seen since leaving the United States. Lights were on, an extravagance during the day since they were powered by generator. A huge freezer and a modern stereo with a row of monitoring lights occupied one wall. The bathroom had not only running water but also hot water.

We were introduced to a woman named Constance, who wore a pantsuit, beret, and lipstick. I pressed my hands down my limp skirt. Godfrey offered us schnapps, which we declined. He obviously thought this peculiar but nodded and poured glasses for Constance and himself. I don't know where he got the liquor; I hadn't seen any since arriving in Ghana.

He was working on an agricultural project, he told us, waving vaguely at a long table covered with books and maps and a few plant specimens. He had been trained in Austria and had just returned the year before. His first assignment had been this project. In well-modulated English, he added that it had not been his idea to be assigned to this "godforsaken part of the country." Both he and Constance came from southern Ghana.

Godfrey stared morosely into his glass and then beyond the windows, his glance flickering over the beautiful landscape. He asked what we were doing in this part of the country and was surprised when Mary said that she lived here.

"But is there electricity or water where you live?"

"No."

He looked shocked. "How do you live?"

Mary laughed. "Oh, I manage. It is not that difficult."

Godfrey looked agitated nonetheless. "Really, this is horrible. We have visitors like yourselves come all this way, and then we treat you like this. It's shameful. I myself find this place nearly unbearable; to think that you, who are used to so much, should have to live like this."

"You needn't worry," Mary said. "I've lived here for twenty years." She hesitated. "It is harder for me to go home now than it is to stay," she admitted.

He looked at her incredulously. "For twenty years? What have you been doing?"

"I translate the bible."

"You are a missionary."

"Yes."

He smiled and put down his glass. "Well, I admire you. I could not do it."

"If it were up to me alone, I couldn't either. But the Lord gives us strength to do his will."

He nodded, gazing at the table. Then he changed the subject. His camera had broken, he told me. Would I look at it? I found the problem to be a dead battery. He asked if I had an extra battery to give him, as none were available in Ghana, but I had only the one in my camera.

"No more pictures, then," he said flatly.

"I'm sorry."

He shrugged. "It is of no account." But he was ungentle as he shoved the camera back into its case.

We parted soon after. As I glanced back, I saw the well-dressed pair standing in their doorway—Western lights shining behind, African dust swirling ahead. They watched as we, dodging the goats, jounced down the dirt track.

Mary and I soon drove through a large town. While less central than Tamale, this town was busier. Pedestrians and vehicles clogged the road. The occasional herd of wrinkled cattle wandered through, their hides hanging in dehydrated folds about their necks. The huge market teemed with traders, unlike the one in Tamale, which had been leveled by soldiers.

Shops lined the streets, their only advertisement the large painted signs hanging above them. We drove by INTERNATIONAL WATCH DOCTOR, LIBERATION CHEMIST, OTIS AND GUYS TAILOR SHOP, and CALIFORNIA BARBERSHOP. Paintings drawn on the barbershop illustrated the hairstyles offered. Each had the name of an occupation below it. Underneath a picture of a balding man with a neatly groomed goatee and heavy black glasses was the word "Professor." A close cut was entitled "Soldier" and another with heavy sideburns, "Barrister." Down the street a large sign identified the eating establishment below it: DON'T MIND YOUR WIFE CHOP BAR.

In front of the permanent cement shops stood kiosks—small plywood shacks. They sold everything from vegetables to reggae cassettes. An italic script over one ramshackle kiosk proclaimed ALHASSEN'S PHARMACEUTICAL COMPANY, but like most of the kiosks it was boarded up and the word QUIT had been scrawled in red by soldiers.

We stopped at the post office, built by the British half a century before. The foot-thick walls sported a millimeter of whitewash as protection against the weather and those urinating. The red post office box standing outside was inscribed with a crown and "E II." The last mail pickup from that box had probably been a decade earlier.

Inside, it was cool and dark. The high ceiling and sweep of tiled floor accentuated the cavernous quality of the building. The wooden counters were dingy with layers of polish. In response to our request, a lounging clerk told us they did have stamps that day. The world championship soccer stamps were the most popular. Other stamps depicted local birds and plants, or commemorated steps made in the nation's development. Recently the price in the corner of each stamp had been covered with a smudged black star. In the opposite corner, with the same fuzzy ink, a new number represented a 200 percent increase.

When we emerged, I paused beside a woman cooking on the bottom step. She hiked her baby up her hip and continued stirring plantain in a woklike vat of red palm oil. She did not return my smile. Her baby held her drooping breast between both hands and, sucking, stared at me askance. I bought some of the slices enveloped in red pepper sauce. The woman wrapped them in a smooth green leaf and I overpaid her, delighted with how easily certain foods translated me back to childhood.

We continued through the town, passing a lorry park, where trucks adapted for public transportation picked up passengers. Along one side, taxis without tires rested on blocks of cement. Along the other side were vehicles parked in a gas line. None of the vehicles had drivers, indicating that it would be some days before gas was expected.

A truck exited as we passed. Its worn tires were so badly aligned I could see their angle. The truck listed, and the people inside sat crushed together. Others clung to the top of the cab and the baggage on the roof. Across the front in bright orange was written AFRICAN PERSONALITY. This slogan was old; coined by Nkrumah, it had gone out of vogue. Another rare one was NEVER DESPAIR. I had seen it last on a rusted hulk, sunk up to its axles in mud and abandoned. Now one saw WHO IS FREE?, ENOUGH IS ENOUGH, and WHO KNOWS TOMORROW?

Our trip was a long one. The potholes, indirect roads, and police barriers at each town kept us on the road for the better part of the day. We stopped at the home of translators working in the Mampruli language, and at the mission hospital in Nalerigu, leaving mail in both places. Near dusk we arrived in Dosau, the village where Mary lived.

We rounded a corner on a small rise, and the plain lay before us. I could see the stream the road crossed and then the clustered compounds of the village. On the far side, I could detect a long building which I guessed was the school. The compounds were grouped evenly on either side of the road. In the middle of the village spread the cleared market area. On the near side rose the white building of the church. All around the village, fields stretched. It was in between the harvest season and the planting season, a dead time, neither here nor there, with the leftover stubble from the previous season still poking up.

As we drove down into the village, we slowed to part a herd of goats whose smell steamed from their matted coats. Mary halted between the church and a compound. In the failing light, its mud walls had taken on the warmth and texture of human skin. Each was marked, like the people, with regular scars.

In northern Ghana, people lived in compounds—circles of huts. Mary's compound was typical in having three round huts with conical thatched roofs and a shoulder-high wall that linked each hut to the next and encircled a courtyard in the middle. Her compound also had a rectangular hut with a tin roof.

The compound belonged to Jafok, the village pastor and Mary's co-translator. He also owned another compound at the other end of the village, so he lent this one to Mary.

I unstuck myself from the plastic seat and got out of the pickup. I was gritty from head to toe. A crowd of children had appeared, Africa's ever-present public relations. The bolder children smiled, dipped their knees, and softly greeted us. "You are welcome."

"Thank you," I replied.

One of the younger boys pushed his way forward and stuck his arm out. "I am pleased to meet you," he enunciated. The others giggled. They had probably learned the greeting in school.

I took his hand. "I am pleased to meet *you*." He grinned, stepped back, saluted me, and, making a smart turn, returned to the others.

I started to lift my bags from the truck, but two boys relieved me of them. I stood there, disconcerted, hoping that it was my status as a stranger, not my pale skin, that had prompted them. I would have felt better taking the bags myself, but doing so would have been misunderstood. So does our history haunt us.

After they unloaded the bags, the children transferred the water Mary had brought with her to a barrel in the compound. Good water was difficult to come by. When water could be found, it often carried diseases like cholera, typhoid fever, and schistosomiasis.

I stood watching the children work, entranced. The

sun hung low in the sky, blushing orange-red through the veil of dust. Some of the precious water had anointed the boy heaving the bucket from the barrel. His young, lithe body was entirely dusty except for the patch on his shoulder glazed with water. He turned on the truck bed, and, mouth pursed, muscles taut, bent to hand the dripping bucket to his companion on the ground. The dying sunlight glanced off his shining shoulder. The contracting muscle swelled beneath the slick skin as if it were myrrh rising to kiss its kindred liquid—water. Living water.

The boy straightened and, catching my eye on him, beamed. I shook myself, startled, as if I had seen the changing of water into wine.

Mary and I took stock of the compound. The thatch roof of the bathhouse had blown off into the courtyard, leaving the tepee of sticks that supported the thatch bare. Its brown order framed the compound across the road. Unraveling thatch and bits of straw had scattered over the shiny surface of the packed dirt floor.

Ants had invaded one of the rooms. A large pile of clumped dirt marked their presence. Such ants were impossible to eliminate, so Mary simply shut the door on the empty room.

Bending like Ghanaian women, we swept the compound with short brooms. Described in a local riddle as "a hundred soldiers wearing one belt," the brooms were made of pliable twigs tied with string. I was not used to sweeping bent, so my back tired quickly. Afterward, Mary and I bathed and rinsed out our clothes. My once white T-shirt appeared rusty with dust.

Mary's home—the rectangular hut with the tin roof— had two glassless windows covered by wooden shutters and a wooden door that opened on the compound. All her worldly possessions could be found in that room. She owned a minimum of furniture, and the dozen boxes stacked along one wall held largely materials for translation work. Most of the boxes she had not unpacked. I wondered if she did not need them or if she wanted to be ready to leave at a moment's notice.

Everything in the room was covered with plastic to protect it from the harmattan dust. Mary uncovered only her camping stove and tiny refrigerator. Other than her manual typewriter, these were her sole appliances. She gave me a cot and a mosquito net to set up in one of the huts. There weren't many insects out at this time of the year, but a mosquito net protected one from the small animals that might fall from the thatch.

In the evening, by the light of the small kerosene lantern, Mary looked weary. She remained silent as she prepared a small meal with the supplies we had brought. Her sure, deliberate movements belied her tired face.

While she cooked I examined the room, committing it to memory. A clothesline, on which dish towels and clothing hung, divided the room. On the wall over her bed hung a church calendar which featured a picture of that church's board of directors; all male, seated, and somber. Mary had written in above the coming Sunday the note the evangelical calendar lacked: "Epiphany."

Next to the calendar stretched a huge colored poster that struck me as out of place. It depicted a tiger recoiling after slapping a still pool. The movement had been so quick that the photograph caught the crown of water but not the tiger's paw. It was already halfway back to the tiger's side. My eyes went back again and again to that astonishing feral grace. When I asked Mary where she bought it, she said it had been up when she came, so it probably belonged to the pastor. The calendar and the poster were the only items hung on the standard white-washed walls.

After dinner we cleaned up, throwing the dirty dish-water out the window above the dinner table, a wonderful convenience.

Mary then uncovered a trunk, tugged two sheets from it, and began to make her bed. I straddled one of the two wooden chairs and rested my folded hands and chin on the chairback.

"Do you ever read in the evening?" I asked, watching her, making conversation. Only translation manuals were to be seen.

"Not usually."

"You said you liked to read biographies when you were young," I prompted.

"Yes." She snapped the sheet out over the bed.

I waited. "I suppose it's hard to come by books out here."

"Mmm." She tucked a corner.

"Do you ever bring books from Tamale?"

"Sometimes."

I straightened. I was anxious for a response. "I read biographies when I was young, too. I've given up on them, though." I paused, but she said nothing. I plucked a napkin from the table and smoothed it over my knee. "They always disappoint you. It's like evolution: no one can explain exactly how that first fish made the transition from water to land. It's just a mystery." She had stopped making the bed, but I didn't notice. I was folding the napkin into ever smaller squares.

"It's the same with biographies," I said. "There's always this inexplicable leap in that person's life. A leap from the familiar where the rest of us live into that foreign place where fame or fortune is just a matter of walking long enough. It's as if they turn a corner. Something coalesces, something different than does for the ordinary person. One moment they're trapped in the water, the next they're breathing air."

I looked over to where she stood by the bed, a pillowcase dangling from her hand. "I'm always hoping I'll find that leap explained, that I'll be told what corner they rounded. But every time I reach that part of a biography and I'm hoping that this time they'll tell me, that they'll give me a clue so that I can escape the water too, the

37

biographer starts speeding up, and before I've turned the page I've read, 'and she was an overnight success,' and once again I've missed it.

"Take David Livingstone," I continued earnestly. "What made him go to Africa? I don't mean his missionary zeal or whatever, but what made him think of it? Did he read a book? Did he see a poster? Did he overhear a conversation? If so, why didn't the others there react the same way he did? One moment Africa was just a word to him, the next a continent to be explored."

Mary was staring at me. I became embarrassed and stopped speaking. I replaced the napkin on the table.

She tucked the pillow under her chin. "Actually," she said, pulling the case on, "I find it difficult to read by the kerosene lantern."

I nodded without speaking. Then, as the silence stretched, "Your eyesight is poor?"

She placed the pillow at the head of the bed. "When I was home I had it checked. Unfortunately"—she gave an apologetic smile—"I have a touch of river blindness."

"River blindness?" I repeated with disbelief. Onchocerciasis is a dreaded African disease transmitted by biting flies. "That can't be cured. I mean, your eyes just get progressively worse until you go . . ." I stopped, hearing my bluntness.

"I'm just hoping I'll be able to finish the work," she said simply, smoothing the sheet with one hand. "It's getting harder and harder to do the proofreading."

"I'm so sorry."

She smiled again. "It's only to be expected, I suppose, after living here so long. Most of the older people have it."

And I sat, silenced, while she deftly pulled the bedspread up and finished making the bed.

As we prepared for bed—a surprisingly complicated task without lights, running water, or a toilet—she offered me

38

a lantern. "You can use this," she said, turning its wick down. I stood in her doorway, a towel over one arm.

"I'm all right. I can see the way with my flashlight." I waved it and smiled.

She extended the lantern by its slim handle. "But you'll be needing this for later."

"Why?" I didn't want to be pampered.

"Don't you sleep with a light?" She leaned toward me, searching my face.

I smiled in defense against whatever weakness she looked for. "No. I'll be fine."

She looked doubtful. "Are you sure?"

"No problem," I said, making a deprecatory gesture.

She straightened. "Well, make sure the net is secured properly."

"Thanks," I said, turning to go.

"And check your shoes and clothing in the morning before you put them on. Scorpions hide in dark places."

"Thanks. Sleep well."

In my hut, I lowered myself to the narrow army cot and tucked the mosquito net under the edges of its pad. The scrabblings in the thatch above were of no concern now. I left the door open so that the evening air would cool the hut, which had absorbed heat all day. From the small window in Mary's hut came a low glow.

In the middle of the night I awakened chilled and rose to close the door. During the harmattan the weather changes dramatically from hot in the day to cold at night, just as it does on the desert whence the winds come. The sky had cleared of some of the dust, and I could see the slow-wheeling stars above the outline of Mary's hut. The miles stretching above were dark and deep. In the distance the faint murmur of drums sounded like the ocean. In the village all was quiet.

I turned to go back to bed but was astonished to see what appeared to be a village on fire. About ten miles away, something lit up the entire horizon. It even slightly illuminated the wall of my hut. I looked around to see if anyone else was watching this spectacle, but no one was. Suddenly, the arc of light heaved up over the countryside, lurched to the right, and lurched back. Memories of imaginary childhood worlds rose to my sleepy mind, and I wondered if I had been abruptly translated to such a place.

Then, on the crest of the rise we had come over, about two miles away, a truck appeared. In that expanse of blackness, its standard headlights were the source of incredible light. Only the people who walk in darkness can see a great light. I waited for the truck to reach the village, and a few minutes later it did, rumbling by with a hiccup of its gears. By its beams I deciphered the legend across the cab of the truck: EVERYTHING BY GOD.

The following morning I woke early. I rose, careful not to tip the precarious cot, and entered the compound on my bare feet. At that hour, the dust had diffused the low sun to an orbless glow.

I washed my face in the bathing hut. The water was cold and refreshing. Dew filmed the metal bucket. Through the sticks of the de-thatched roof I surveyed the village. The red-earth huts seemed tongued into flame by the early sun. A few pigs rooted in the earth, and the chickens were already at their incessant scratching. In the distance, beyond the village, were hills layered with rock and scrub trees.

After breakfast I wrapped a towel around my shoulders to keep myself warm, Mary put on rubber boots to protect her feet from snakes, and we went for a walk. The few people we passed had wrapped their sleeping cloths tightly around themselves. Not many were up. On such mornings people did not rise until it was warm enough to take the customary bath.

The children were awake, though, and they chased

us, shouting "Heh-low" and drawing back, at once delighted and terrified, if we turned to greet them. They
clapped their hands when they elicited a response, just
as children do when they get a reaction at the zoo.

The compounds on either side of the road were not
of homogenous design. More expensive huts had tin roofs
and wooden doors. Most had thatch roofs and thatch doors.
One compound, made in a neighboring area's style, had
no outer doors at all. A shoulder-high wall completely
enclosed it. To get in one climbed over the wall by way
of a notched log.

In front of this compound, I saw a cooking pot resting
on a forked stick. The three-pronged stick, embedded in
a patch of cleared ground, rose to waist height. Two flat
rocks slanted at a rakish angle on top of the pot. Sand-
wiched between the rocks was a long, thin stick and about
the edges of the pot dried a white substance. Mary told
me that it was "juju." She questioned one of the boys in
the local language and then told me that this particular
juju kept "lizards," that is, thieves, away from the house.

Nearing the other end of the village, where the pastor lived, we decided to greet him, even though it was
early.

Mary had told me about Pastor Jafok on the drive
to Dosau. He had been working on the translation longer
than Mary. Before she came to work in the Bimoba language, two Englishwomen had been translating with Pastor Jafok. Because of illness the women had had to go
home, and the work had stopped before completion. When
Mary had finished her first translation—the Konkomba-
language New Testament—she felt called to help Pastor
Jafok finish the Bimoba translation. Konkomba and Bimoba were somewhat related, as much as French and
English are, so Mary thought she could be useful. Her
praise of Pastor Jafok was quiet, but I could tell that she
admired him.

"He is very good at translating," Mary had told me.

"He is faithful and always ready to work. He has a remarkable ability to make a translation natural sounding and clear."

Mary went on to talk about how people like Pastor Jafok were changing the way the bible was translated. Mary's first translation had been done the old way, using a technique developed for South America, where her translation group, Wycliffe, had first worked. There, a translator became fluent in the language and then translated the bible. This process often took fifteen to twenty years, because the languages had never been studied and lacked orthographies. The translator checked the translation with the people and questioned them to see if they understood it properly, but otherwise the translator worked alone. This method had been needed in South America, where many of the indigenous groups had no educated members. Since no members knew a language into which the bible was already translated, such as Spanish or English, they could not help with the bulk of the work.

In Africa, education had been more widespread. Most tribes, especially in Ghana, had at least a few members who had been educated in French or English. This made the task easier. Ideally, in such situations, the foreign translator provided expertise and advice, and the indigenous speakers who understood the language being translated did the actual translation.

The director of the institute at that time was an American who had brought together a group of village men acknowledged by their people as splendid speakers and trained them to write the translation on their own. I had watched them at work once, and walked away astonished. Some of them had a few years of education but nothing like the level thought essential for such academic work. These farmers surrounded themselves with dictionaries, concordances, and exegetical works that most native English speakers would have found difficult to read and, with hands that still held pencils awkwardly,

43

churned out the New Testament in record time. An indigenous translation like theirs has a different quality than one done by an outsider.

As we drove, Mary expanded on this idea. "If the bible is translated by someone who understands both the biblical and the African cultures, the imagery can be put into terms that people understand."

"Such as?"

"Well, in Asian cultures they have been translating the phrase 'I am the bread of life' as 'I am the rice of life.' "

I nodded. "That makes sense."

"It's more accurate too. In Asia, life without bread is commonplace. Life without rice is unimaginable. I think that's closer to what Christ was trying to say."

Someone like Pastor Jafok, then, was a godsend. Not only was he literate in English but he had been trained at a bible college and was familiar with the text to be translated. Furthermore, he was a Christian interested in volunteering his time and resources for such a task. Mary and Pastor Jafok worked together through every step of the translation. African and Western, they labored side by side, leaping from one language to the other with easy grace, building a structure from the materials of both cultures. Mary's first translation had taken over fifteen years. Her second would take less than five.

The road emerged from the clustered compounds of the village into the fringe of scattered compounds. On the left, a small ridge exposed slate like lopsided steps. A dust dervish picked itself up, shook itself out, and spun along the road until it folded, breathless, on the shoulder. Where it fell, we turned off the road and walked toward Pastor Jafok's compound. Except for one other, his compound was the farthest out.

Close to the compound, we called for him, as was the custom. Strangely, no one came out or called back. The compound had not been swept in several days. The mud walls were eroded and the thatch untidy. The compound needed to be either abandoned or restored. Mary called out again, but still no one came. We were just about to leave when an adolescent boy came out and greeted us in English.

About fourteen, he was short with lovely, smooth skin. In his features still tarried the roundness of childhood. One of his eyes was red and running, but he gave us an astonishing smile.

"Hello, Bijabo," Mary said. "Is your father home?"

"No, madame. My mother is there. She will come and greet you?"

"Yes, please." Mary looked puzzled. Bijabo left to get his mother, whose name was Saamo.

She came out with her sleeping cloth wrapped over her shoulders. She clasped it to her, arms crossed over her breasts, her fingers denting her upper arms.

On meeting her, I realized the source of her son's beauty, if not his smile. She greeted us quite solemnly. In fact, at first I suspected that she had been crying. But I assumed it was just a Western misinterpretation of facial expressions.

She had the same high, round forehead as her son. On both cheeks a long diagonal scar indicated that she was not from this tribe but from one farther north. She had a triangular nose, strong, even teeth, and sparse, arched eyebrows.

But it was none of these characteristics that lured my casual glance into lingering. Something about the beauty of young African women catches me unaware. It comes not from a particular symmetry or shape—some static notion of aesthetics—but rather from a presence lent them by the women who stretch behind them in time. A Western woman's face speaks only for herself. An African woman's face speaks to me of her mothers. In every contour, in every hollow of an African woman's face dawns

45

her silent heritage. This beauty does not survive well the drudgery of endless tasks and continuous childbearing, but it remains ancient and timeless in the line of women.

While I studied Saamo, she and Mary exchanged greetings in the local language. Then Mary said, "Your husband is not here. Has he traveled?"

Saamo looked away. "No."

Mary hesitated. After a pause she spoke. "We will see you in church?"

"Yoh." Saamo glanced from Mary to me. She turned away. "Till tomorrow then."

"Yes. Bye-bye."

We walked toward the road. I concentrated on the path, wondering what had disturbed me about their interchange. Mary walked ahead, and I sensed in her back a stiffening that went beyond her usual posture. We had just turned onto the road when a movement caught my peripheral vision.

A figure came running from the compound next to Pastor Jafok's, the compound farthest out. He ran quickly, gracelessly. A rooster flew, squawking, from his path.

We stopped, and as he reached the road he slowed. He was about thirty-five, a thin, distinguished looking man, though haggard about the face. His nostrils flared in an aristocratic manner, as if he were always aware of a piercing smell. The distinguishing tribal marks that Saamo had were absent from his face. He wore shoes.

"Hello, Miss Mary," he said, approaching us. "How are you?"

Mary started to turn toward him but did not face him fully, forcing him to speak to her sharp profile. "I am fine, Pastor. You are well?"

"Yes."

Mary examined her hands. "And your family?"

"Fine." One was required to respond this way regardless of the circumstances.

Mary glanced at him. "I do not think that you knew

46

that I arrived yesterday afternoon. You did not come to greet me."

He gave an abashed smile and answered the question with oblique courtesy. "We will start work on Monday?"

"Yes, if you can come."

"Oh, I can come."

Mary introduced the two of us, giving his name as "Pastor." Then he returned the way he had come. We stood, two figures on a dirt road on the edge of an African village, and watched as he walked away.

We turned back, and Mary shook her head. "Something is wrong."

"What do you mean?" I sensed something peculiar but did not trust myself to judge such things yet.

"Did you see Saamo? She had been crying."

I was surprised to have my judgment confirmed.

Mary continued. "And why was Pastor not at home? It's a cold morning. I hardly expected them to be up."

"He seemed to be coming from the neighboring compound. Perhaps he had gone to fetch something," I responded. "Though I suppose Saamo would have asked us to wait."

"He must have known that I was home. It's only customary to welcome back a neighbor."

"Maybe he was busy."

Mary smiled. "That is a Western excuse, not an African one. There is always time for social responsibilities like greeting someone."

"What do you think is wrong then?"

"I don't know." Mary tightened the African cloth around her shoulders. "I do know that whatever it is, it has been going on for a while now. When I returned from furlough, they had both lost a lot of weight. I asked Saamo if she had been sick and she said no. She's usually so vivacious."

We walked in silence then, and my attention turned to my surroundings. The children ran ahead, jostling each other and steering various handmade toys with wheels. The older children carried their younger brothers and sisters. I spotted a girl, too young to own any clothing other than underpants, with her hip thrust out and an earringed child resting with her arms about the girl's throat. They both stared at me.

Every time the girl went anywhere, she took the younger child with her. She would do so until the child was old enough to fend for herself. This care produced a strong bond. I later heard elderly people introduce with gratitude an older sister or brother as "the one who carried me."

Just off the road, still on the village's outskirts, someone had started a new compound. It was the time of year to be building new huts or rethatching old ones: before the rains, so the walls could dry, but when there was still enough water to make mud. If families had grown during the year, new huts were added to old compounds. The compounds expanded or contracted in response to the needs of the family, a paradigm of the African community.

On the right we passed the house with the juju out front like a mailbox. It was almost behind us when a young man named Ninkpo emerged and in English invited us to visit. He was a farmer who sometimes helped Mary with various tasks. He wore only shorts; the muscles of his body were sharply demarcated beneath glossy skin. Hair traced down his belly, and when he turned, I saw that his spine was a deep groove. Later I learned that he was blind in one eye.

We climbed the log and descended into the courtyard. Seven huts made up the compound, each capped with a metal pot. We greeted the head of the household and his two wives, who sat on low chairs. They and the children were eating a bit of cold food before the regular meal was prepared.

All the adults in the household—Ninkpo, his father, and his father's two wives—had their own sleeping huts. In the small space between each sleeping hut and the next were bathing areas. Twice a day people bathed with a bucket of water collected by the women, a bar of soap made from animal fat, a fibrous gourd dried to a sponge, and a cotton cloth used to dry off. The floor of the compound and the walls of the hut had a slick surface, which did not absorb water because of its special mixture of mud and dung.

A cooking hut prevented the women from having to cook outdoors during the rainy season. Outside this hut lay pots for water and cooking, as well as a grinding stone. The grinding stone consisted of two parts—one stone shaped like a tablet with a hollow eroded into the top, the other like a rolling pin without handles. The women knelt on the earth, strew grain across the tablet, and ground the rolling pin over the grain.

In the next two huts were earthenware jars larger than men, which stored the grain harvested the season before. Against the outside wall of the granary hung a bag made of furry animal skin. Seeing my interest in it, Ninkpo said that his family had once used the pouch for keeping juju. He reached in and pulled out a bicycle light. They now kept bicycle parts in it.

We continued on then, and a little before Mary's compound we came upon the market. A low fence enclosed the rows of wooden stalls. At this early hour, nothing much was happening, but soon it would be flocked with people. The sellers, mostly women, had already settled in place. Many had a child at the breast. They watched us as we came into the market, their legs straight on the ground, and spoke sotto voce to one another as we passed.

49

Food items made up most of the wares: yams, to-matoes, leafy vegetables, onions, and a few small green oranges. Local soaps, cosmetics, and juju items were jumbled together: powdered eye shadow in goatskin vials sold among the turtle shells. Some women served fast food, that is, ready-to-eat stews. Western items were conspicuous by their absence. I saw no bicycle parts, matches, or spools of thread. One stall had a few used Western clothes. Such clothes were called *charlie wawa,* which translates as "the clothing of dead white men." Villagers assumed that living people did not discard wearable clothing.

In a special concrete building with mosquito screening, the butchers plied their trade. Despite the screening, the place was murky and fly infested. Entrails and slabs of meat lay in heaps. Muslims cut their meat elsewhere in the market, according to strict procedures. Pito, the local beer, was sold outside by the calabash—a kind of gourd—and dipped from a cool earthen jar.

Mary approached a woman selling apart from the others. When the woman saw Mary, she smiled. A gold-threaded red scarf framed her old face. She was from a distant tribe; her forehead tattooed with a fading design of blue crosses. A lattice of wrinkles edged her eyes. She talked while Mary selected some green onions from her small bunch.

As I stood there, trying to see something besides the villagers' eyes watching me, I spotted Bijabo, the pastor's son, coming toward us. I was struck again by the freshness of his face and that smile. Mary finished her conversation with the woman and paid for the onions. Then Bijabo, Mary, and I continued to the compound.

Bijabo was a student at a secondary school in Tamale, I discovered. Although only fourteen, he attended the equivalent of the eleventh grade. He had entered secondary school early. I asked him what he planned to do, and he said that he liked languages because of the trans-

50

lation work his father did. He wanted to attend the University of Ghana to study several. He hoped to travel to Togo so that he could practice the French he was learning. I wondered whether these ambitions were distant dreams or real possibilities.

Reaching Mary's compound, Bijabo told Mary that his mother had sent him to ask if she might talk with her. Mary replied that Saamo should come by anytime. He smiled and returned the way he had come.

"Is he their eldest?" I asked, watching him exit.

"Their only."

"Really?" It was rare for African women to have only one child. I followed Mary into her hut.

"He's their firstborn," she said. She placed the bunch of green onions in the tiny refrigerator and retrieved a bottle of water. "They have tried to have other children, but Saamo always miscarries."

She poured two glasses of water and handed one to me. "She has had several miscarriages. Two children she brought to term died in infancy. Finally, she had a hysterectomy. She would probably have died during the next pregnancy."

I shook my head. "That must be difficult for her."

"Being barren here is not to be a woman," she stated flatly.

Startled, I examined Mary's face, but she said no more. I finished my water in silence.

Mary set up her work table under the shade of her hut's thatch overhang. She worked on her translation at one end, and I worked on writing about what had happened so far at the other. My diligence about writing did not rise simply from the need to put together an article for the newsletter. A careful record of this visit might become a map for my own journey. And yet, though I tried to capture Mary on paper, she eluded me. Her reserve was not easily broached, and the superlatives that rose to my mind carried me too far beyond her. She, in contrast, was working steadily, stopping only to make proofreading marks. Just before giving up and closing my notebook, I scrawled as an afterthought, "Pastor and Saamo—intriguing."

After lunch I went to my sleeping hut to rest. The circular room was bare except for the narrow cot canopied by its mosquito net and my suitcase open on the floor. I folded the net back on itself and lay on the cot.

I ran my hand along the red-pebbled surface of the wall and then along the smooth floor. Light spilled through the cracks in the wooden door, and mustiness emanated from the thatch.

The wood sticks of the thatch supports formed a spider's web. From the circular wall of the hut they led like spokes to the apex of the roof. They were not lashed into place but simply leaned against each other. It was remarkable, then, that they supported the considerable weight of the thatch. Strengthened by their communal meeting at the top, the sticks needed no bindings. Alone, each stick could not have supported even its own weight. Tilted together they supported a weight far beyond theirs.

The thatch consisted of long grass woven into tight water-shedding mats. These huge mats were laid like shingles on the stick frame. Unlike roofs made of tin, thatch roofs do not leak.

Awakened by the call visitors made when approaching a compound, I turned on my side to look through the door's crack. Across the patina of the courtyard, Mary still sat in the shade next to her hut, proofreading. The rest of the courtyard was exposed to the sunlight. Straight ahead, between Mary's rectangular hut and the two round huts, was the gate into the compound.

Through the gate came a boy leading an old, blind

woman. He walked slowly, grasping the end of a cane, which she also held. She was bent like a question mark, her face bunched with age. The boy guided her to a seat several yards away from Mary. As was the custom for conversation, especially formal conversation, she did not sit next to Mary.

After the initial announcement of her approach, the woman had been silent until she sat down and waited a polite moment. Then, averting her eyes with respect, she clasped and unclasped her hands. Rocking forward, she started the local greeting, forgetting none of the required courtesies I learned later from Mary. She inquired after Mary's husband and children, although she knew that Mary had none; asked how Mary found the day, if the traveling had gone well, how the work was. Mary responded to each question, the two of them bowing and almost singing the greeting. The words tumbled over each other, neither woman waiting till the other had fully stopped, the ancient call and response needing no pause.

With neither of them looking at the other or waiting for the other to finish, I wondered if either cared for the other. Both the questions and the answers were stock phrases. But the greeting was dictated by ancient traditions that valued what appeared rote to me. Because of the traditions, the women bridged their disparate cultures and marital status with momentary ease. The familiar greeting bound them together, just as its strict formality acknowledged the distance that lies between all people.

I rose, dressed, and crossed the courtyard to greet them. Ninkpo had come by, too. He stood with relaxed stance just inside the gate.

I nodded at him and greeted Pokper, the blind woman, dipping in respect as required. She held my hand between her two. Life had eroded lines into her hands that ran like emptied riverbeds across the parched surface of her skin. Her sightless eyes turned toward some spot above my head. Smiling, she made a comment to Mary. Mary did not respond, except for a perfunctory smile.

"What did she say?" I asked Mary, twisting my head to look at her.

"She said that my heart must be white."

"White?"

"It is the way here of saying that I must be happy. She thinks that my daughter has come to visit me."

I laughed, pleased by the association. "Did you tell her that I was not your daughter?"

"No."

Pokper spoke again. "She says that you should stay in the village," Mary translated. "She will teach you to grind grain and pound yams and carry water. Then she will find you a fine husband."

I laughed again. "Tell her that I am not strong like her daughters." But Mary shook her head. The polite offer demanded no response.

I crossed to sit on Mary's bench in the shade. During our conversation, as the afternoon waned, the sun sank, and the eaves gave less and less shade. The line of hot light rose up our bodies, a steady encroachment on our comfort.

Mary folded her hands on her orange dress. In contrast to Pokper's carved hands, Mary's had veins that stood out like welts. Ninkpo leaned against the wooden post that supported the extended eave. Only his head rested in the shadow. The old woman sat in the full sun. Mary and I faced her from the shadows.

Mary told me they had been speaking of Pastor. I thought back to that morning, and his face as he had asked about starting work.

"Did you find out what was wrong this morning?" I asked.

Her voice was cleared of any emotion. "Well, I cannot

be sure, of course," she said, "but it seems Pastor has taken a second wife." She gestured toward the old woman nodding in the sun. "Pokper here has been telling mo."

"A second wife?" I was shocked, even though it was a common practice. "But isn't he a pastor?"

Polygyny—marriage to two or more women at the same time—was the traditional pattern of marriage in northern Ghana. Nevertheless, most Christians felt it an important, if difficult, tenet of their faith to remain monogamous. In particular, many churches required pastors and elders to have only one wife because Paul specifically dictated this for church leaders. Furthermore, many young non-Christian men chose to avoid polygyny as the culture became more Westernized. For these reasons, it was quite unusual for a young Christian pastor to take a second wife.

"Yes," Mary answered, "he is a pastor, and someone whose judgment I've always trusted." Although the words were regretful, her tone had no inflection.

"What happened?" I asked, as if the question could be answered. Ninkpo was not close enough to hear our quick, quiet English. Pokper did not understand English at all and sat unmoving in the hot sun, waiting for us to finish our private conversation.

Mary explained in the same controlled tone. The news had not completely surprised her. She knew something was wrong between Saamo and Pastor. A second wife was not the news she had expected, however. For some time people had been saying that Pastor would take another wife because his first was barren. One child alone could not care for elderly parents or insure the continuation of the family. But everyone knew that Pastor couldn't take a second wife and remain a pastor in his church.

Consequently, Mary had ignored the rumor. She was confident he would not jeopardize his position as a pastor.

For fifteen years his life had been based on it. But the news Pokper brought put everything in a new light. The previous week Pastor had sent a piece of paper to the church saying that he was resigning.

Mary continued, "No one has heard that he's taken another wife, but that is the assumption."

"Maybe it's the wrong one."

"If it is, I can't imagine why he would have resigned."

I gazed at her, trying to read in her face how she felt about this information. She looked away, as if I was sitting too close. The line of sunlight had risen past her feet. Some clay, gathered during our walk that morning, stuck to the edge of one rubber boot.

"Don't they know for sure whether he has another wife?" I asked, thinking of how small the village was. "It would seem an easy thing to identify."

"Apparently she hasn't arrived yet," Mary replied. "Besides, it is not the custom here to speak directly of things. It's possible no one knows. They say that Saamo got up and ran weeping from the church when she heard the announcement of his resignation. I gather that it came as a surprise to her."

"Or she wanted to make a statement."

Mary nodded.

"Hmm." I leaned forward to examine the eroded floor beneath my feet. The slick surface was pocked, and red dirt showed below like a wound. I felt a growing curiosity. What was going on? Was a story about to unfold?

"I'm sure they are not telling me everything," Mary continued. "People will be reserved because these things should not be brought up in front of a stranger like yourself."

I became brisk. "Well," I said, "it looks like you'll have to go to Pastor and find out the true story."

Mary's mouth compressed, as if she had tasted something bitter. She stared at me, then turned away. Ninkpo, Pokper, and I watched her from our relative distances.

She sat very straight, looking far across the fields, a sailor used to gazing at horizons.

"I don't know," she said. "They have a saying here: You must strike at water before reaching the fish. It seems fairly clear that he has taken another wife. I think it is time for me just to go."

"Go? Why would you go?" I was confused.

"Well, I can't work with him any longer."

"Why not?"

"Pastor knows that having more than one wife is wrong," she asserted. "It will only hurt the translation to have someone working on it who has deliberately sinned."

"But you haven't heard what he has to say," I protested.

She replied sharply, "It is clear that he feels inadequate to continue in the ministry: his marriage is disintegrating, and he can't face me. I don't need to know anything more than that." She stopped. And I don't want to either, I finished.

Attempting to sidestep the uncomfortable silence, I asked Ninkpo a question. The sun shone full on him now, and I could see the easy sweat standing on his face.

"What do you think about this second wife, Ninkpo?"

He glanced at Mary and then shrugged. "If a man does something that he himself knows to be wrong, and if he tells his people that it is wrong, then who can blame him?"

"It will bring him no happiness if he knows it is wrong," Mary retorted. "He will only regret it."

Ninkpo did not respond to this remark, and there was another silence. Searching for a different tangent, I asked Ninkpo how the women here felt about having co-wives.

"They will like it. If there is only one wife, she will be working so hard. She has no one to go with her to fetch water or to be helping her with the husband."

"Does Saamo feel that way?"

"Oh, no," he said, as if the question was absurd. "She will like being the only wife."

"What will she do now, then?"

He shrugged again. "What can she do? Can the wind carry a stone?"

Mary spoke very softly, "There is a wind that can carry any stone."

We all fell silent, and after a time Ninkpo took his leave. Pokper soon followed suit by calling to her guide, who came from where he had been playing outside the compound.

Mary and I remained outside. The sun had sunk to the horizon, and the first of the cool evening winds had begun. I leaned against the sunbaked wall of the hut, enjoying the heat against my back. I glanced at Mary. The line of sunlight lay across her groin, neatly dividing her body in half and making the orange dress glow. Her hands lay open like shot birds.

I found her gaze fixed on the baobab tree rising from the field beyond the village. The veil of dust between us made the tree seem more distant than it was. The baobab was immense, probably hundreds of years old, gnarled and gray. It stood in outline against the sky, the sole survivor of centuries of grass burning and wood gathering. Scars appeared along its bulges like arcane orthography and soon it would bear a fruit that was both sweet and acidic.

Mary spoke, the quick anger gone. "When I came back from furlough, he seemed like a different person. I could not put my finger on what it was, though. I just felt uneasy with him."

"When did you come back from furlough?"

"I have been back about six months."

"And he hasn't said anything to you?" She shook her head. "That seems odd."

58

The pinched expression returned, and she replied indirectly. "We were translating one day, and I finally just asked him straight out, 'Is there anything between you and the Lord?' I told him that I felt something was hindering the work. He asked me if I had heard anyone saying anything against him, and when I said no, he was silent. I told him that I felt something was wrong and asked if he wanted to talk about it.

"He was silent, and then he said that he had intended to talk to me. I have not been here in Dosau much," she explained, "since my furlough. So he has not had much of an opportunity." She paused. "I moved to close the book, but he said, quickly, no, some other time we would talk. Well, that other time has never come."

Her sudden release of reserve astonished me. I had not heard her speak at such length before.

"I would never have claimed that I knew Pastor intimately. That wasn't my job here. We were working to translate the bible. And as a language helper he was one of the best. He was so faithful and so committed. But still, I would have thought he would have said something to me. We've worked together for several years." She paused.

I barely breathed. The sparks of stories are so easily snuffed out.

Mary spoke again. "You can live in this country for so long and still be . . ."

I supplied the needed word. "A stranger?"

She looked at me, startled, as if she had been surprised by the sound of my voice. "Yes. Yes. That's what I meant," she said. I had the sense it was exactly what she hadn't meant. She raised her hand to her hair with a distracted movement.

From a distance, I examined her. How strange she must appear to those here—childless, husbandless, far from her own people, showering her life on lifeless paper. Even her God was a man without children, wives, pos-

59

sessions, land, or subjects. And yet, how strange she must appear to those at home, too. A woman left behind: her fashions from another era, her way of speaking odd, her relationships attenuated by a lifetime of separation. She belonged to neither world; each considered her a part of another.

Soon after, we left our bench, and Mary methodically set about preparing the evening meal. She gave me two plantains to peel and slice for frying. It did not seem the time to reopen the topic of Pastor, so I asked a related question.

"How do you feel about this whole issue, I mean of one wife?"

The topic of polygyny occupied our conversation during tea. The issue defied any attempt to simplify. They who state their case first seem right, until others come and examine them. Each point contradicted the next. The old questions all clamored for answers. How did Christianity translate across cultural borders? Which of the biblical injunctions were necessary to the life of a Christian, and which had been intended only for specific circumstances?

Some felt that men who had more than one wife before converting should keep them. Some felt only elders and pastors should be restricted to one wife. Some felt decisions about what was right should be made on an individual basis after considering all the variables. Others disagreed with these views, saying that polygyny was not acceptable in any form. They cited the passage about "the two shall become one."

Although the ratio of women to men was almost equal, polygyny worked in Ghana. The men often married at a later age than the women, and they married women of a wide range of ages. Women returned to their families and remarried if their husbands treated them badly. To recommend that men be monogamous would mean that

60

some women would not have husbands. Since a woman's status stemmed from her husband and children, this would be a hardship.

After tea we returned to the bench outside. Night had fallen. From where we sat, surrounded by the protective walls, we could see the first stars.

Mary spoke. "Do you know how they describe the movement of the stars here?"

I shook my head.

"They say, 'The stars go walking.' "

I tilted my head back. "That's beautiful."

In the cool of the evening, I asked naturally about the translation. The events of the day had made me less formal. What made her keep going, I asked, even when it was difficult?

She answered simply. She wanted to finish the New Testament and make it available to the people. "Lives are being affected by it. People are really coming to know the Lord. I see such a difference in the people who become Christians. The love and the joy they have for each other, even those who are not from their tribe, is beautiful. People are becoming a part of a larger family."

Mary explained that in this part of Ghana there had been tribal conflict. A few years before, many had been killed in a war between the Konkomba and the Bimoba. The Konkomba—the group that Mary had first worked with—had always been considered barely human by surrounding tribes, and the stigma had made them aggressive. The Konkomba had little power at the national level; few of them were educated, and even fewer had the kind of Western economic security that some aspired to.

A friend had told me that he was once at a prayer meeting where a Konkomba man had been asked to pray. He had stood up hesitantly and started to pray in Twi, the most commonly spoken language in Ghana. "God in heaven," he said, "we thank you for all the things that you have made. But you know that I do not speak Twi well. And I know that you do not speak my language. So I am finished. Amen." And he sat down.

Then someone arrived to study their language. People were amazed that Mary had come from so far to learn Konkomba. When they found that their language—the most intimate part of a cultural identity—was worthy of being written down, they began to change the way they viewed both their language and themselves. Thus, the message of the New Testament began to have a real effect in an area that had had churches for years. So has Christianity always depended on translation.

Cam Townsend, the man who had founded Wycliffe Bible Translators, was once asked a question that challenged him for the rest of his life: "If your God is so great, why doesn't he speak my language?" Questions like this impelled people like Mary to show others that God did speak their language.

We had fallen silent in the darkness. Into our silence came the sound of women singing on the other side of the village. Sounds carry clearly in a place where there are no telephones, no stereos, no televisions, no traffic. I asked Mary what the women were singing, and she listened for a moment before answering.

"A traditional song. It says that if you use this certain kind of soap, it will attract the young men."

I laughed, comforted that the foreign song dealt with such universal concerns.

Across the street a child started to wail but soon stopped. Then, even the women fell silent. The only sound was of the drums in the distance, so far away that the rhythms were lost and the sound merged with the dark surroundings to become the sound of the earth itself.

The next morning, Sunday, I awoke to the call of a dove. The unexpected but familiar sound brought the world outside my hut in. I could see her through the crack in the door. She turned her head sideways, and the light hit her moist eye and black-ringed neck. She dropped her head to rearrange some feathers on her defenseless breast. Then she was gone.

Because the morning was cold, church would start late. After breakfast Mary used the extra time to do some chores around the house. Since she enjoyed listening to the BBC every night before going to sleep, fixing her radio was a priority. She brought the radio out and laid it on the table under the eave of her hut. Alongside the ancient green radio with its rounded contours, she laid her make-shift tools.

With a cloth reserved for the purpose, she wiped her glasses clean and placed them deliberately on her nose. She set to work systematically, searching for the fault. The sure movements of her hands demonstrated that she never grew impatient with the inanimate.

I watched her as she worked with focused attention. The painful questions of yesterday seemed forgotten. I wondered whether she had resurrected them the previous night as she lay down in that half-packed room. Did the dilemmas of the day tease her sleep away, or did she pass them smoothly into the hands of the Almighty? So much of her I could only guess at.

For the previous two days I had questioned Mary and had walked away with nothing more than general facts. No epigrams on life among strangers. No stories of strange miracles God had wrought. She did her work well, but she seemed to have no passion for it. She had lived most of her life alone, but she had no particular advice on how to accomplish that feat. She had affected many lives, but she had no sense of her own uniqueness. I wondered how someone who had dealt with the very texture of language for so long could find it so difficult to communicate. She had started to open up about Pastor, but even then it had seemed like she hadn't known what she felt. How was I to know what to do, if she didn't? I hadn't much time left.

Mary took the screwdriver between her hands and loosened a screw. I sat on the edge of the table, facing the courtyard, swinging my legs. My hands lay idle in my lap, a callus raised by the pen the only mar on their smoothness.

I watched Mary examine the radio by running her fingers over its parts. "You're like a pioneer, Mary. Doing so many different things."

Mary looked pleased. "I've had to learn. When I came here, I had never even taken a flashlight apart." She loosened another screw. "Most of the women who are single have had to learn to do things for themselves."

She began to speak about her first experiences in Ghana. As I had hoped, her concentration on the radio enabled her to speak without self-consciousness. When she slackened, I asked another question, eager to hear more.

In 1962 the main office had been in Accra, five hundred miles away from them, she told me. Since Mary and her first partner, Marge, had no private vehicle, they always took the public transportation. Using this system meant walking long distances and waiting long hours. Not much had changed since she had ridden the buses then. They were more crowded now, and the drivers often omitted the horn blast made before a bridge to warn playful spirits away.

Then Mary and Marge bought a Honda 50. "When we got it, we felt like free people." Mary shook her head with a faint smile. "We must have been a sight! That tiny motorcycle would carry us, our suitcases, and our tins of petrol for hundreds of miles." They scooted by village compounds, children staring at what was hardly more than a bicycle burdened with two dusty white women and their bulging luggage.

As might be expected, the motorcycle tended to break down. They were always getting stuck on some dusty road between towns. Then they would prop the bike up, pull out a jug of water and the owner's manual, and settle down to deciphering the instructions, which had been translated from the Japanese.

"Every time I got that manual out," Mary remarked, "I would pray, 'Dear Lord, don't let my translation be like this one!' " She looked up with that rare smile of hers, and we both laughed. I felt close to her.

"So you can see how I would have to learn to do these things myself." Mary peered into the dark interior of the now dismantled radio and selected another tool.

I rubbed my hand along the worn wooden table. "Mary." I hesitated, but the shared laughter made me bold. "Why have you never gotten married?"

She replied, to my surprise, without hesitation. "Because of the work."

Paul had been right, she explained; to devote yourself truly to the Lord's work you have to be single. The man she had thought of marrying disliked the idea of overseas work. So the choice was clear—mission or marriage. She chose mission.

"Have you been glad that you made that decision?"

"For a woman to really be a translator, she can't be married."

"Why not?"

"So much diverts you from what you have committed your life to do. Most of my partners have gone home. If I had been married, I would have had to leave, too. The work would have gone undone then."

I nodded. "Have you ever personally missed being married, though?"

She raised a hand to her eyes, but I did not retract the question. I knew that I was prying, but my need to know overcame my politeness. What enabled someone to live so completely alone? An answer lay somewhere, I was sure, a reason for Mary's strength, something that her methodical approach to life could not account for, something that her full sense of humor could not produce, something that just being Christian didn't explain. Some key that would fit the lock of my own life.

My pressing was to no avail. Mary changed the topic slightly, and her answer brought me no closer to the mystery. "Margaret," she said—identifying a former partner of hers—"says that being married is no more difficult than being single; it's just different."

She released her tool. "I am not going to be able to fix this radio," she stated. "I'll have to take it into Tamale." She screwed the panel back and set the radio aside.

From inside, she brought out a bench that needed its leg reattached. She turned the broken bench against its brother and laid several nails in straight lines. Lightly gripping the end of the hammer handle, she selected a nail. Then she spoke, as if she knew that I had not understood.

"There are many things that you learn," she told me, moving the nail into place. "Being punctual is not important here." She began to tap the nail in, her speech as staccato as the hammer. "So, after a time, you learn not to be tried by it. Or to try to change it." She examined her work. "I've learned how to accept other people from the way the Ghanaians have accepted me and my strange life. But many things you never come to accept."

Mary spoke frankly. "It's very difficult living with just one other person in an isolated situation for a long time. It knocks off rough edges and corners."

Relationships like those shared by translating partners rarely occur in other situations. Lives intertwined at every level. Each of Mary's partners had been the only person who really spoke her language and the only person who shared her cultural context. The two were constantly together—living, working, relaxing. Often Mary hadn't met her partner until she arrived in the field. Sometimes her partner did not even share her cultural background: Mary had worked mostly with Americans.

"Someone in the administration once told me that he thought any two Christians could live together." Mary shook her head. "Perhaps in a better world," she added.

Ghanaians exerted inadvertent pressures as well. Many saw foreigners as having endless material goods. People wanted things that Mary had but couldn't give to everyone. If she gave a skirt to a special friend, others were insulted. Should she give nothing to anyone and risk being thought stingy? Or should she give to some and risk angering most? Or should she give everything away and guarantee impoverishment?

A foreigner was constantly unsure how to behave with the wealth that she automatically had. Knowing that whole cultures had been destroyed by the introduction of Western products didn't help much when a pregnant woman asked for a steel machete to ease the task of clearing her farm. Her human sense overcame her historical sense. And, fittingly, history made necessary tasks odious, as one of Mary's early partners had found.

Gretchen was going into town when some people begged for a ride. Gretchen explained that the car was full, but when they insisted they could fit, she allowed them to come.

Gretchen had been sick with malaria and was still tired. At a critical moment, she was inattentive to the road, and they crashed into the undergrowth along the shoulder. One of the passengers became hysterical. Her baby had been crushed to death, she screamed. She accused Mary's partner of attempting to hurt them.

As it later turned out, the baby was not dead. Everyone was fine. Still, the experience was overwhelming for Gretchen. Several had nearly died, she felt, because of her unwillingness to refuse to do a favor. The burden of caring for other people was too much.

Differences in cultural behavior also contributed to the strain of living. Westerners need privacy. For a people who live mostly outdoors, this need is difficult to understand. The children didn't understand why Mary or her partners became angry when the children hung over the walls watching them do nothing but type for hours. Should they continue to chase the children away day after day? The repetition bored only into their own sense of self-worth rather than into the children's propensity for hanging over the walls.

"You're public property, like 'Lady Di,' " Mary said. "Only she gets training in how to handle it."

We were silent for a while. Mary continued to work on her bench, while I digested the information that Mary lived within these constant tensions. I considered her twenty years of battling them alone and was moved. Such courage.

I found her watching my expression. I looked away, across the compound, dusting the table with my hand.

The heat of the sun had taken the edge off the morning. Its height translated the world into abbreviated shadows. Someone nearby hammered with an even, rhythmic stroke, unlike Mary's. Tap-ta-tap-tap. Pause. Tap-ta-tap-tap. Pause. The rhythm makes the work pass more quickly. In the distance, ticking like a typewriter, I could hear the small gasoline engine of a mill translating the local grains into life-sustaining meal. The mill's onomatopoeic name, *nika-nika*, fit it.

"Did I tell you about the fermented Fantas?" Mary asked with a smile.

"The what?"

"The fermented Fantas."

"No."

Mary selected a nail. "It used to be that we could buy Coke, Sprite, and Fanta Orange in the town of Yendi. My first partner and I would make the trip out once a month to buy some."

They did not have the motorcycle then. In the morning, as they walked out to the main road, one of the children carried their suitcase on his head. They sat on the suitcase and waited by the side of the road until a lorry came. If it didn't arrive by that evening, they walked home and returned the next day.

"We would play Scrabble and get sunburned while we waited. We loved Scrabble. Every Friday evening the two of us would turn up all the kerosene lamps, make candy and popcorn, and play Scrabble. Once, I remember, the BBC played some of the old dance music we knew." She laughed. "Gretchen would sometimes make that American candy, what is it? Fudge?"

I nodded.

"And we would drink the Fanta or Sprite we had bought." She paused, remembering, and then continued. "One time we got a case of Fanta that was slightly fermented."

"You're kidding."

"No. It is not entirely surprising, considering, but Gretchen wrote a letter to Coca-Cola in the United States. She was happy here then, and it was a funny letter. Here she was, far from home, and the one thing that seemed to be a little bit of home had failed her. She sent it off and we forgot it. But her letter did more than we thought it would. About a month later, a red-and-white truck pulled up on the dusty path in front of our compound. I've never been more surprised. It had come all the way from Kumasi."

"No!"

"Yes. That's about four hundred miles. A local manager and a photographer got out. The manager was 'very sorry.' He asked us please not to send any more letters to the U.S. as they had 'troubled him too much.' Would we please take these new crates of Fanta and allow them to take pictures of us drinking Coca-Cola? Later we got a letter of apology and some of the pictures of us smiling and drinking Coca-Cola."

I shook my head, laughing. "I can't believe they came all this way."

Mary nodded. "I always wondered what they used those pictures for."

She hammered the last nail into place and ran her hand along the joint. She turned the bench over and sat on it to test it.

From where Mary sat, she could see a man ambling up the path to the church. She pointed him out to me. He walked with his chin forward. Just outside the church a carburetor hung from a wooden post. He hit the carburetor with a metal rod several times—our first call to church. Then the man returned the way he had come. Mary told me that he was the chief's eldest son, Batbik.

He was one of the bright young men who, caught between the traditional and the modern, had tired of village life and left for the city. Things went badly for him in Kumasi. Finally, Batbik came home. He started going to Pastor's house and through Pastor became a Christian.

"He hasn't been the same since he left, though. I think it was too much Indian hemp," or marijuana. "He trained as a teacher. He's a farmer now." She sat for a moment and then stood.

"Should we get ready to go over?" I asked. Saamo had said she would be in church. Perhaps she would talk to Mary then.

"Oh, no. Church won't start for quite some time. And even then, we won't go until they call us."

"How come?"

"The service goes on for three hours. We don't need to be there for all of it."

When someone from the church finally called us, it was afternoon. With the church right next door, though, we had heard the singing going on before then.

The church was a rectangular building about the size of three mud huts in a row and had a wooden door at one end. Low windows with wooden shutters ran along both sides of the building, letting in shafts of light. Inside, narrow school benches spanned either side. The women sat on the left and the men on the right. In front, opposite the entrance, a foot-high wall marked off a semicircle of ground. Inside this area rose a ledge for the speaker to sit on and an altar, both made of hardened mud like the floor. The altar also served as a lectern for the preacher and was covered by a white cloth.

The church service had no set liturgy, but it followed a rough pattern. Singing alternated with praying for about an hour to an hour and a half. At any moment I might have been called on to pray, a fact that encouraged me to be alert. Next, people danced forward to place their offerings in the straw collection basket. Finally the sermon was given, lasting at least an hour. Then, after the blessing, the service was over.

That morning we entered when the singing was in

full swing. Several men were playing square-framed drums, and two women were shaking gourd rattles. Everyone clapped. Those acknowledged as good clappers set up counterpoints of rhythm. The song master was passionately conducting the congregation in the Twi song "*Anwanwa do ben ni*," that is, "What a wonderful love." The mud walls echoed with sound.

When a song ended, the song master shouted the only words I was to hear in English, "Praise God!" To which the congregation replied loudly, "Amen." The call and response was repeated several times in quick succession. Then someone would start another song, and everyone joined in. Sometimes a particularly fine singer was asked to call, and everyone would respond to the leading.

A song, once started, could continue for twenty minutes, but not because it had a great many verses. "*Anwanwa do ben ni*" had only four lines to it. Mohammed, a Ghanaian friend, had once told me that the purpose of singing was different for the African than for the Westerner. Westerners sing songs with many words in them, he told me, but they do not fully understand all those words when the song is over. "As for us, we will sing the same words over and over again until we know them." Africans sang until the spirit and the meaning of the words were fully realized. Out of the repeated language welled a joyful response to its truest meaning.

We moved to stand in front on the women's side, next to Saamo, who was exulting in the music. She smiled as we approached. Pastor stood behind the altar with the preacher for the morning, a local bible student named Emmanuel. Pastor was wearing a tropical suit that in Africa is worn by men of any nationality and a certain status for semiformal occasions. I was surprised to see him there, but no one else seemed to be. He carried his body easily, but his face was set and reserved.

After the singing and praying ended, the bible student gave the sermon, using as his text Philippians 3:12–16—forgetting what lies behind and stretching forward to what lies ahead in Christ. Mary translated this much for me. Then I was on my own.

Emmanuel wore platform shoes that added about three inches to his already impressive height. The lapels of his brilliant white suit had a wide blue border. In one hand he carried a large bible, which he never opened, having long ago memorized the relevant passages. Behind him a sign plastered crookedly to the wall declared, SAVE THE LOST.

I did not understand a single word Emmanuel uttered, but by the end of his sermon I understood Philippians 3:12–16. Language communicated only a part of his message. The pitch and decibel level of his voice communicated another part, and body language another. The passage on which he spoke was suited for this style.

Every time he spoke of "pressing on toward the goal for the prize of the upward call of God in Christ Jesus," his hand went up and his voice went down. Lowering his hand and raising his voice, he rolled forward, ending in an explosion of sound and movement. Emmanuel turned to the left and shouted a question. The answer came back from the congregation, "No!" He turned to the right and shouted a question, and the answer came back, "No!" He faced straight ahead, his whole body straining forward, his hands reaching out, his blue-edged lapels leaping from their white background, and shouted a question. The congregation shouted back, "Yes!" Emmanuel twisted to look over his shoulder and shouted; again the answer, "No!" He moved to the back and crouched, both hands straight out, whispering fiercely to the congregation, looking neither to the left nor to the right nor to what lies behind but only pressing onward. By the end, I felt I was hearing Paul himself speak in those tumbling, impassioned sentences.

At the close of the sermon, he scanned the congregation, then eyed each of us in turn. He asked us to stand and pray together.

Everyone stood and began to pray out loud to God with his or her own prayer. We spoke together but individually, each voice working within and against that of the community.

Saamo had seemed fine until this point in the service. As she prayed, her speech slowed, the words becoming fewer and fewer until she was only rocking back and forth. Then tears came. She pushed past me and left the church. I looked at Mary, wondering if someone should follow her, but no one did.

After the blessing, church ended, and we went outside. I was introduced to some of the congregation. One member was an old blind man, a victim of river blindness, who had spoken frequently during the service and had often started the songs. His face, creviced and brown as a walnut, fascinated me, and I asked to take a picture of him. Through the lens of my camera, I could see one misty eye open, unseeing. In the other socket hung only an eyelid. His infirmity, however, did nothing to weaken the strength of his face. He gazed above and beyond my shoulder, as if he saw something astonishing that we could not see. He told me, through Mary, that he thanked God for the opportunity that came because of his blindness to preach the "good news" at the weekly eye clinic.

Batbik, the chief's son, and Emmanuel, the bible student, came up to shake my hand. Emmanuel grinned, now looking more boyish than prophetic.

"I enjoyed the sermon very much," I told him, knowing that he would speak English because of his training.

"Thank you. We are doing what God has called us to do. We are witnessing to his glory, and we thank him that he has chosen us. Yes, the harvest is plenty, but the laborers are few."

Everyone nodded seriously, except for Saamo. Standing nearby, she spoke up flatly, "Now even those who had been harvesting are resigning." No one smiled in acknowledgment of her dark humor.

At that point Pastor, who had been out of earshot, approached from the other side and asked Mary if he might speak with her. I looked at Saamo. She had asked to talk to Mary first. Perhaps Pastor had heard of this request.

Mary shaded her eyes to look at Pastor. He stood stiffly, but not self-consciously. Mary brought her hand down, straightened her already straight back, and nodded. The two started toward the gate of the compound.

I thought it best that they talk alone, so I asked Batbik if he would take me to the stream to photograph. When he said he would, I hoped for a chance to hear from him about Pastor.

We walked down the red dirt road that transected the village. Tires had worn rough and pebbled ruts into the road. Between the ruts rose a smooth ridge and along the edges of the road a fine silt collected.

Outside the village, on the side opposite from Pastor's compound, we passed the baobab tree that Mary had gazed at yesterday. Three women walked ahead of us. They had basins on their heads, their shoulders and buttocks thrust back. They were going to collect water. A group of women bearing water came toward us, a rapt attention on their faces to the unseen burden on their heads. The women smiled as they swayed past.

We talked as we went along. I asked Batbik if he knew Pastor well, and he said he did. Then he started to tell me his own story, the one Mary had given me the bare version of. At first, the story seemed disjointed, but eventually I was able to understand.

Batbik had been trained as a teacher and had had a good job in the area. Then he had become "too fond" of Indian hemp, or marijuana. He was not at his post often enough, so he lost his job. He traveled south in hopes of making his fortune, but jobs were hard to find then. "Now it is somehow better under this new government, J.J.'s," he said, "but then it was bad."

One day Batbik asked a friend to give him a bottle of whiskey so that he could bribe a man to hire him. In the end his conscience would not let him "corrupt" someone, so he decided to kill himself by drinking the whole bottle. Three days later he woke in a hospital. Batbik told me that as a result of the incident he had lost some of his faculties.

The chief's son had no choice then but to come home. He remained in despair. He kept smoking. "No one would be my friend. In fact, I had a quarrel with this, my last friend. That day I said I will go and greet Pastor." He visited Pastor even though they had not been friends before. Pastor gave him a Billy Graham pamphlet entitled "The University of Life." After that Batbik often visited Pastor's house, and they discussed religious matters.

We had reached the stream, leaving the grass for a sandy patch. Batbik stopped and turned to me. Framed by the still pool behind him, he spoke earnestly. "Eh, I had been wasting so much. I had been finished. But I came to know the great love of God for me. The Lord has given me life when I was dead. Jesus is really a friend when we are alone."

I nodded. "So Pastor was the one who led you to Christ?"

"Pastor is a fine man. There will be some who will be whispering things against him, but as for me, I will never." He shook his head vehemently.

I examined his smooth face—the curve of his black ear, the hair cropped so close that skin showed. I thought of how he groped for words, feeling his way through his own story as if he had wandered into some unfamiliar town. His face gave voice to what his tongue no longer could—that his future was the casualty of an ancient collision. Batbik gave me a guileless smile, and I smiled back.

Several women had gathered near us. They stood on the dry, flat rocks around the pool. One was helping another to put a basin of water on her head. The woman accepting the basin crouched, her hands above her to receive the weight. The other woman planted her feet and straightened with the basin's weight, straining with her back and arms to place the burden carefully on her companion's head. The woman stood, making the water slosh but not spill.

After I took pictures of the women, we returned to the compound, speaking of other things. Beside Mary's compound I took both Batbik's hands in mine and thanked him. He nodded, his eyes clear, and ambled away.

Inside, Mary and Pastor were still talking. The tableau they formed against the textured wall of her hut was rigid with tension. Mary sat straight on the bench she had fixed that morning, her hands clasped in her lap. Pastor leaned forward. His forearms rested on his knees; his head hung down. They spoke in the local language without looking at each other.

I went to my hut and, while I folded some clothes, watched them. As in the sermon, I could not understand what was being said. It is odd to watch two people communicate, to hear their words, but not to understand.

Pastor talked more. Mary listened but gave no verbal encouragement. Occasionally she asked a question as if she were throwing down a gauntlet. Pastor's voice was always even in response, continuing whatever he was saying as if no interruption had occurred. Sometimes after a question, however, he forced himself from his bent posture and stretched. But as he continued to speak, he settled into his previous position.

I watched his face as he spoke. Again I noticed the

77

arched nostrils. His hair was well cared for. His teeth were even. While his face seemed ascetic, his body, appropriately lean, was too relaxed for asceticism.

Pastor stood. Mary continued to sit, and when he spoke the parting words, she nodded her head but did not speak. His hand was on the gate when he turned and asked Mary a question. I heard the English word *petrol*.

A silence fell as Mary stared at Pastor. The silence stretched until Pastor uneasily looked away from Mary's gaze. She still did not answer. Finally, with a brief, helpless gesture of his hands, Pastor turned and walked out the gate.

Mary crossed the courtyard to my hut and asked if I would go for another walk. I nodded.

We took a different path than Batbik and I had, so we ended farther downstream. The streambed was about the width of a road. Five feet below where we stood on an outcropping of the bank lay the stream. Actually, so little water ran through it could hardly be called a stream. The water stood in stagnant pools linked only by trickles. The algae rose thickly. Surrounding the pockets of water were dried-up sandbars and rough rocks. During the rainy season, the water surged through the bed, tumbling rocks along with it, but the dusty banks gave no promise of that abundance now.

As we turned to walk along the bank, I saw a huge waxy flower. It sprouted up like part of another world. As big as a football, it grew in two halves on the ground. Where the halves parted, I could see a blood red, hairy interior. Mary said it trapped insects and digested them. The same land that produced the tiny yellow bloom also fostered this flower, which was more animal than plant.

The winding footpath along the bank led us away from the village. With every footstep, dust rose about our ankles.

"What happened?" I asked, removing the weight of expectation from my tone, although I longed to hear what Pastor had said.

Mary sighed, but her tension went unrelieved. She then answered my question. As was appropriate in matters of great importance and delicacy, he had started the conversation by approaching its subject indirectly. He asked Mary whether she knew of his resignation. She answered that she had been told and that the news had surprised her. She had thought his work was the most important thing in his life. He replied that the pastors on the church board had made the same comment. They had tried to persuade him not to resign, but Pastor told them that he had personal reasons for doing so. He did not tell the pastors what these reasons were.

A silence fell then; both knew what had to come next. I imagined that Mary hesitated to ask the needed question, unsure if she really wanted to know what would follow. In the end she told him that she would need to know about these personal matters. If they disqualified him from being a pastor, they would probably disqualify him from being a translator.

Then he began the long story about taking a second wife, although he did not mention her until well into the story. He started, instead, with his first wife.

As a child Saamo had had periodic epileptic fits. They became much worse when she was pregnant. For this reason, she kept miscarrying. Pastor believed that Saamo's mind had been affected. He went on to detail incidents that supported his claim. She often had violent tempers. Once Saamo and another pastor's wife had fought by the stream. What the fight was about he did not say, but they fought until neither of them had clothes on.

I broke in. "That doesn't sound like Saamo," I protested. I thought of the quiet woman we had met that first morning, standing alone with her arms pressed across her breasts. Then my mind swung to the weeping Saamo at church and her bitter humor. Perhaps I didn't know Saamo well enough to say.

Pastor had named other disturbing events. Once they had been visiting in a neighboring village, and Saamo had become angry. She fought with the pastor of that village and even bit him on the neck.

I was shocked into laughter. "That hardly seems possible! What kind of person would do that?"

Mary shook her head. "I don't know. I should think I would have heard these stories before. I usually do. And yet I suppose they could be true." Mary added that it was possible that the seizures had affected Saamo's ability to reason, causing her to do violent things.

Mary was picking her way over a rough spot in the path. I paused before asking my next question. "He wouldn't lie to you, would he?"

"No." Her answer was neither hasty nor hesitant. "No, he wouldn't lie to me." Of all the things Mary said about Pastor, the sure confidence of this answer lingered with me longest.

"So," I asked, "what did he say was the point of these stories?"

"He claims that she is impairing his job as a pastor. No one will come to his house because she is so disturbed. They all avoid her. Because of her he cannot properly carry out his ministerial tasks. Therefore, he would like to find a wife who is easier to live with."

I made a derisive sound. "If she's sick, he should be helping her out, not kicking her out."

"Well, there is always her family to help her." Mary stopped. We were far from the village now, surrounded only by the small, crooked trees that managed to grow at the water's edge. A hill pushed up on the far side. Beyond it I could see nothing through the haze. No sounds carried from the village.

80

Mary bent to place a hand on one of the large rocks of the bank and lowered herself to it. "It's just ironic," she observed when seated. "He wants to send Saamo away because she is hurting his job as a pastor, and yet now he isn't a pastor."

I sat on a rock below Mary's. Silently we looked over the stream.

"I asked him, 'What about the marriage vows you made before God?' He told me, 'Well, you make your vows, praying that you can keep them, but if you cannot, you cannot. At this time, it is being worse than the worse they talk about in "for better or worse." ' He said that the marriage was very unhappy."

I shook my head and picked up a pebble. It was rough and dusty, but I rolled it up and down my palm.

"A couple of times," Mary added, "I wondered if they were happy. But I never asked."

Mary plucked a long blade of grass. Once, she said, Saamo had been gathering some fruit that had fallen from the papaya tree just outside Mary's compound. The tree belonged to them, just as the compound did. Saamo had let the fruit grow too ripe, so it had fallen and bruised.

While she gathered the fruit, she said to Mary, "Oh, my husband will beat me!"

Mary had responded, concerned, "I don't think that he beats you."

And Saamo had replied, "Oh, no! It is an expression. He has never touched me."

Mary turned the blade over and ran a finger along its rib. "I never saw anything that told me otherwise."

"Hmm." I pulled my arm back and flung the pebble across the stream. "It's amazing what can go on without your even knowing it."

Mary looked at me sideways with a peculiar expression. Suddenly I felt exposed. I looked away, afraid that I had revealed my thoughts about her.

After a moment, she continued. "Only once was there any hint that things might not be what they should be. But I didn't think much of it at the time."

Saamo had suggested to Mary that Pastor would take a second wife, but Mary had not believed her. When Mary voiced her disbelief, Saamo said that he would do it without thinking twice. He had stopped sharing things like his radio with her. Expecting Mary to understand the ramifications of this event, Saamo stopped there, shaking her head.

When Mary said she did not understand, Saamo told her that Pastor's decision was the first step in his taking a new wife. When a man has more than one wife, she explained, he can't share with all of them. Therefore, he stops sharing before a new wife comes. The old wife can't then say her husband's actions are because of the new wife.

At that time, however, Mary had felt that this interpretation was only Saamo's rather than the common belief. She assumed she was hearing one side of a quarrel between Pastor and Saamo.

Mary stood and laid the blade of grass on the rock. We started toward the compound.

"So, what else did he say?" I prompted.

"That was most everything."

"He didn't say if he had actually married another woman or not?"

"No."

"Hmm," I said. "I hope everything works out." Mary didn't respond. She looked exhausted, as if talking required reserves she no longer had.

"By the way," I asked curiously, "what did he say, right at the very end, when he was about to go?"

Mary's voice had been open, but the uninflected tone returned. "He wanted some petrol. He has a small motorbike which he uses for the work. It's been a great help to him in getting out to remote places that needed the

Word. Usually I bring petrol for him, as it's next to impossible to get it here."

This statement hardly seemed a full explanation. I examined her face.

"You seemed upset."

"He didn't want the petrol to do the work. He needed it to visit his 'future wife.' "

Her voice was like a gavel. Nothing further could be said.

Approaching Mary's compound, I noticed a crowd had gathered. People stood facing the church and the field beyond it. As we came closer, I saw Saamo talking with three of the young men of the village. They lounged around Mary's truck.

Bent at the waist in a girlish pose, Saamo rested an elbow on the edge of the truck bed, cupping her chin in her hand. She was laughing. The vivaciousness that Mary had mentioned was apparent. Saamo seemed like another person from the one who had run out of church.

When Mary approached her, Saamo playfully put a hand on Mary's arm and gestured toward the crowd.

"Oh, Mary," she said, Mary's name sounding melodic and whole in her mouth, "these people are being foolish."

"Why?"

"Some of the small boys are saying they have found"— she fumbled for the word—"a, this thing . . ." Then she supplied a word in the local language. She continued in Bimoba and gestured toward the field. She finished her explanation by breaking back into English: ". . . fear go catch them."

"I will go look. Come with me," Mary added, but Saamo stopped laughing and appeared nervous. She shook her head.

As Mary and I moved toward the field, I asked Mary, "What's going on?"

83

"Saamo says the children claim to have found an aborted fetus."

I covered my mouth.

Mary glanced at me. "Yes." She continued with a nurse's clinical detachment, "Leaving human flesh out where the animals can eat it is taboo. If it is a fetus, all the dogs in the village will have to be killed. They might have eaten a part of the baby." She searched around her and selected a sturdy stick.

"What are you doing?"

"They want me to determine if it is really human. They can't touch it because it's taboo. Even those who don't believe that it's taboo, like Saamo, are still afraid."

The object was pointed out to her. An old man wielded his cane to frighten the curious children away. They ran from him but only returned elsewhere in the circle of adults. On the dusty ground lay a mucus-covered embryonic sac about the size of a football. I hung back with the others while Mary went closer to examine it, for I, too, was afraid.

Transfixed by the mystery, full of one death or another, I was washed into dim memories of childhood events I had little understood.

My mother and I were in Felix's taxi passing the market in Accra. Felix—the taxi driver who drove us to school each morning—abruptly pulled over, jumped out, and stared over the car at the crowd that had gathered in the market. They had clotted around a particular stall. I could hear people shouting.

Felix ducked his head back into the car and exclaimed to my mother, "Madam, we will stop here small-small time."

My mother had also been watching the scene. She told Felix that he was expected to take us to our destination. While she spoke, he straightened again to look toward the crowd. He leaned back in.

"But madam! They have caught a witch!"

"All the more reason to go on then."

Felix and my mother eyed each other. He had been eager and excited. Now, looking at my mother's face, he seemed to realize to whom he spoke, and his expression vanished. Perhaps, as an urban man, he was anxious not to be caught in a provincial belief. Or perhaps he thought it inappropriate for a white person to see such a thing. Whatever the case, he climbed back into the car and drove on without saying another word.

I turned back as we went around the roundabout. I just caught sight of a surge in the crowd and sticks flashing upward in the sun. And then we were around the curve.

At that moment, Mary crouched to take a closer look at the terrible opaque surface. Still I leaned forward, caught with the others by the centripetal force of death, our breath suspended in our throats. My thoughts whirled back.

During the three years that my family had lived in Ethiopia, I had often awakened from my afternoon nap to the sound of mourning. Clutching a toy, I would hang out the window of my room and see people pressed against the iron gates of the medical college. They wailed and wept while toward them traveled a shrouded length. A high, keening cry sometimes rent the oppressive weeping. Women beat their breasts and pulled their hair. Professional mourners wailed praises in honor of the dead. At first, their abandon terrified me, hinting as it did at some future outpouring of my own. But then, my father told me about an incident at the hospital. In it I saw grief's other side.

One afternoon an old man had carried his ten-year-old son, his only son, into the hospital on his back. When the staff asked the father where he had walked from, he named a village fifty miles away. Between the village and the hospital was a mountain range.

It was my father's first Sunday working at the hospital, so he was unfamiliar with their medical problems. The boy seemed to be functioning normally; he simply became disoriented at times. Sometimes he got on all fours and swung his head, peering at the things around him. My father was going through the routine of examination when the head nurse entered. She glanced at the boy and told my father not to bother: he had rabies. As it turned out, the small scratch found healing on his leg had been caused by a dog.

The father sat in the waiting room. He clutched his homespun cotton cloak tight about him and stared straight ahead. As my father sat opposite the boy's father and looked with his unlined face into the other's furrowed one, he felt helpless. He could not offer those treatments that well-equipped hospitals might. Nothing could be done.

My father's sentences were simple, for the translator's sake. "Your son is going to die." My father paused. "For his last few days, we will make him as comfortable as we can."

The father stirred. "I will take him back to our village."

"I think he will be more comfortable here. We will take good care of him."

"No." His face was impassive. "He should not die so far from his land."

My father consulted with the nurse. "As you wish," he told the father. "I'll give you some medicine to keep the pain from him."

The father nodded. When given the medicine, he did not ask questions. The staff brought his son out to him. His condition was deteriorating. When the boy saw his father, he blinked and his head spasmed away. The father silently gathered him up and adjusted his weight on his shoulder. Night was fast approaching, and it had started to rain. The father walked steadily out the door and through the iron gates on his long journey home.

Mary spoke into the silence, poking the sac with her stick. "This fetus is probably a pig. The uterus is attached, which would be unlikely if it were a woman's. One of the butchers on his way to market probably threw it here after butchering the mother." She asked me if I would help her rip open the sac. I hesitated but then took the stick someone handed me. With it I pierced part of the membrane. Amniotic fluid seeped out. The red dust around the sac blackened with moisture. And again I was in memory of.

During high school, while working at a nursing home, I had watched, for the first time, a person die. I was feeding my favorite patient, Elsie. One of my least favorite patients, Abigail, sat across the room from us. No bigger than a child of ten, Abigail was quite ill and had not spoken for a long time. We had wadded a washcloth inside each of her clenched fists to prevent her fingernails from cutting her palms. Her tensed muscles made her whole body rigid.

The day she had arrived in the nursing home, I had started work there. I was nervous, but Abigail wasn't. She entered fighting. The last place she wanted to be was a nursing home. When I brought her dinner to her, she told me that I could never hope to catch a husband if I cooked so badly. Later that day I walked in and she was crying, curled up on her bed like a child.

"I just want to die," she whispered to me.

Abigail quickly declined. She complained all the time and pinched the aides. We often grew annoyed with her. Still, those times were preferable to the senile lethargy she had sunk into.

Every bite I placed in Elsie's mouth seemed to draw life from Abigail. She grew stiller and stiller. Her eyes

87

followed me, drawing my attention back to her face again and again. I did not feel that she was trying to say something to me. She was too far gone for that. But her stare disturbed me, and I thought of all the times I had not taken time with her. Most patients' charts were full of various comments—favorite foods, special exercises, addresses of relatives. Abigail's chart had none of these notes. Her full name was at the top and near the bottom in a small, neat hand, the word "hopeless." I do not know who had written it; such comments were not standard practice.

As I fed Elsie the last spoonful of Jell-O, I looked at Abigail's face. Her eyes no longer followed my motions. When I crossed to her side of the room, her open eyes still did not move. I put a palm to her cheek. Her skin had that childlike smoothness of age. The familiar purple blood vessels stood out, as if life had lashed her.

With measured step I went to the desk and told the nurse on duty, "I believe that Abigail has died."

The nurse looked quickly at my face and then quietly gathered her things and came to the room with me. She checked Abigail's pulse and breathing.

"Yes, you're right. She's dead."

Is that it? I thought.

"Will you help me prepare the body? We usually clean it before the family comes." The nurse's gaze was steady. "If you would prefer not to, I will see if one of the other aides will help."

I thought of the other aides. "No. I'll help."

And so we lifted her tiny body onto her bed. She had defecated. Cleaning the waste away, I noticed how flaccid her body had become. The contracted muscles had finally relaxed.

We worked in silence, and I kept thinking about how moments ago that face was a personality. I could not have separated that face from who she was. And yet, here was that face, not altered at all, and it was not her in the

88

least. When the nurse and I finished dressing her in a new gown, combing her hair, and closing her eyes, I hesitated a moment before pulling the sheet up over Abigail's still face.

The finality of the movement veiled my memories as well, and returned me to the moment. Mary and I together ripped the fetal sac open. With everyone leaning over us, Mary identified the curled dead life as a pig. The whole village had turned out, and now people walked away laughing, relieved. I watched them depart. The mysterious and dreadful had been beaten back for them, but I remained shaken. Saamo, too, stayed after the others had left, gazing toward the field, one hand palming her belly.

Ninkpo approached Mary's compound shortly after. Mary had asked him earlier if he would take us to greet the chief sometime while I was visiting. Mary knew the chief, but it was inappropriate to visit him without being asked and without escort.

Near the chief's compound stood several huge baobab trees. They shaded a covered area with a raised dais where the chief and his elders settled grievances. After a few minutes, we were granted an interview and invited in. The chief's compound was large because his five wives, and several of his sons and their wives, all lived there. The chief welcomed us outside his main hut, where he sat in a wooden chair with his elders seated on the floor around him. The chief wore sandals, and a voluminous embroidered smock. The elders wore no shoes, and Western clothing. All the men wore Muslim caps. They spent most of the day discussing everything from religion to village matters.

As we greeted them, I made a faux pas that, fortunately, everyone thought funny. The appropriate way to greet someone, especially someone of higher status, is to clap. Not used to such social occasions, I had been watching one of the women, who seemed to be doing something slightly different. Thinking her gesture was what women did in this region of Ghana, I imitated her. Instead of clapping both palms together, I clapped the back of one hand against the palm of the other.

Everyone began to laugh, and I immediately realized what I had done. The gesture I had made was not a gesture of applause but a common way of begging. I clasped my hands between my knees and smiled with embarrassment. My mistakes always came when I was trying hardest. Later, as I left the chief's compound, people were still chuckling at a white woman begging so plainly from a chief. The chief even offered to marry me in an attempt to help me save face.

I volunteered to take photographs by way of recovering from my mistake. The first shot was arranged with the elders seated on the ground, their legs crossed. The chief sat on a small stool. A woman came and, kneeling on both her knees and elbows, held up a bowl of food. A representative picture of a person must include that person's social status. The next shot was of the chief and his wives. The wives were called from where they had been hiding behind the hut. They came and, without any consultation, arranged themselves in a specific order with one sitting next to the chief. I wondered which one was Batbik's mother. Last, I took a picture of the chief alone, by the tree that held the sacrifices he had made to his ancestors.

Then Mary, Ninkpo, and I left, amid many grins, as I said the parting words properly.

When we returned to the compound, I decided to take a bath while it was still warm out. I collected my towel and thick bar of locally made soap and dipped a bucket of water from the barrel. As I stood and bathed in the dethatched bathhouse, I looked out through the tepee of sticks. To my left, the road came down the rise, over the stream, and past the baobab tree amid the open fields. In front, across the road, was our neighbors' compound, from which drifted the smoke of an evening fire, sweet as frankincense. To my right, huts threw long shadows across the road, and there, hidden behind my sleeping hut, lay the now silent market.

The place enveloped me like the water that braided down my body. Longing pierced me. I would be leaving tomorrow, no closer to "home" than when I came, carrying only the memory of this place to mock me.

As I left the bathhouse, Saamo approached our compound with her head lowered. The last piece of the puzzle, I thought. But my eagerness to hear the whole story had faded to uneasiness.

From my hut, I again watched an interchange I could not understand. Mary and Saamo together behaved differently, though, than Mary and Pastor. The two women looked at each other. Mary spoke more often than before, and Saamo's speech was more impassioned. Her voice rose and fell, and she tossed off some words in English.

She was younger than Pastor and full figured. Her face was not thin as his was, but her eyes had the same brightness. Her arched brows made her face appear open, receptive. I watched her. Was she really the unstable person that Pastor claimed?

Near the end of their conversation, Saamo began to cry. The two women held hands and bent their heads for a long time. By the time Saamo stood to leave, the last light was failing. It came over her shoulders and caught her collarbones. Under the brown silk of her skin I thought I could see, even from that distance, the pulse beating in her throat. She clasped one of Mary's hands between her own and smiled awkwardly. "Sister," she said. And then left.

Later, after the evening meal, Mary told me the gist of the conversation. She stood drying dishes as we washed up by the light of the kerosene lantern. Its globe, like everything else about Mary's house, was clean. The cut wick burned without flickering inside the glass, lighting Mary's face from beneath. Her cheekbones shaded her eyes, turning them dark and mysterious as those of an oracle.

Saamo had said it was already too late to do anything. Pastor had married two months earlier. The new wife came from his village. In fact, his mother had raised her. The woman had been given to Pastor's family as a baby to be a future wife for one of the men in the family. Pastor's brother had two wives already, so it fell on Pastor to marry her. Under the circumstances, Pastor had been pressured. His mother went so far as to tell Pastor that the woman would kill herself if he didn't marry her. He was the only one left, according to custom, whom she could marry. To complicate matters further, the woman loved Pastor and wanted to marry him only.

I had expected to hear a very different story, especially from Saamo. I spoke with concern. "Mary, you must admit that information changes things. You can hardly blame him."

Mary selected another plate and dried it carefully. Her voice was not so careful. "When people become Christians in this country, they know what they have to face. If a family is Muslim, they force converts to leave home and never speak to them again. If a family is of the traditional religion, they tell converts that the gods and ancestors which they have not propitiated will harm them. It is not an easy thing to be a Christian. It never has been. There are many things which we give up. Pastor understood that, and he understands that now."

I handed her another dish. "Yes. But knowing what something is going to be like and experiencing it are different. If someone falls, well, who are we to judge them?"

Mary set the plate down and turned full toward me.

"Someone who falls and repents is different," she said, "from someone who falls and does nothing. Pastor is not a young Christian who doesn't know better. This man has been a Christian for twenty years! Yes, there have been many hard times. But never so hard that we fell back on the vows we had made to God."

I nodded. She raised the plate and stared at it as if it were utterly foreign. "Something is happening here which is completely different from in the past." Her voice failed and then filled again. "Things are falling apart for him, and I don't know why."

She put a stack of dishes away before she spoke again. "Saamo said that considering the circumstances she might have tried to live with this other woman. But this woman is not the only one Pastor has been seeing. Last March, Saamo went to a three-month course in Tamale to learn how to teach primary school. It has always been a dream of hers to teach, and she finally had the money and the time to go. When she came back from the course, she found that the mother and daughter in the compound farthest out had practically taken over the house. Pastor had been 'loving' the daughter since May."

"That does put things in a different light." I handed her the last dish, but she did not dry it.

"He goes early to their compound, he eats all his meals there, and he stays there till eleven at night. Long ago he shut Saamo out of his room and hasn't been going in to her. He spent so much money on these other women that Bijabo didn't have enough for school. To make matters worse, Saamo has never liked the two women and considers them slovenly. To have the daughter as a co-wife would be miserable for her."

Mary wiped the cloth round and round the dish. "Even that might be acceptable if Pastor wasn't losing faith. Saamo said that he never prays or reads his bible 'on getting up or going down.' "

Mary put the plate down and folded her towel; her deliberateness seemed to help her keep control. "She asked me to pray with her. Pastor didn't."

She pulled up a chair, and I followed. Now that she was sitting, the light no longer darkened her eyes. Her face resolved itself into its familiar tired lines. Her head hung forward, too heavy for her slender neck.

When Mary continued, her voice was even. "Saamo fears for Bijabo. He no longer has the Christian influence of his father. She says that Pastor has even condoned this family next door doing 'hidden things' for him, by which I understand her to mean juju. She would leave if it was not for Bijabo. It is almost unbearable for her."

"Why doesn't she just take Bijabo and leave?"

"Children belong to the father."

I shook my head. Things were much worse than I had imagined.

And it was not over. Mary listed the grievances Saamo had presented. Saamo believed that it was Pastor's plan to drive her away so that he would no longer be married to two women. Once, when he had told Mary that Saamo had traveled to Bawku on a trip, she had actually gone to the hospital in Nalerigu. He had beaten her so severely, even to the extent of stepping on her stomach, on her "uterus" as Saamo said, that she had had to enter the hospital. He never spoke to her unless others were there. The corn that she had laboriously planted and harvested disappeared one day, and he told her that it was his to do with as he pleased. When she told him that she hated what was happening, he told her that she should leave then.

"Oh, Mary," I managed. "That's horrible."

Mary nodded. "She started to cry today and said she did not know what to do. She was at her wits' end. She said that only God would protect her now."

Saamo and Pastor had met at bible college, Mary told me. Saamo was the only woman studying there—

94

northern Ghanaian women rarely received higher education. She had been very eager and a good student. In fact, if there had been another woman taking the program, she would have completed it. As it was, she married Pastor. She had received some better marriage proposals, but Saamo had wanted to be part of the Lord's work, so she had accepted Pastor because he planned to enter the ministry. She had led many of the bible studies in the village. Now, when she confronted Pastor and said, "I married you because you were a pastor and now you are not," he was silent.

"I just don't understand," Mary insisted. "How could he change so much? He was always so strong and so sure." She looked at me as if I might solve this puzzle. I looked away.

She told me how as a young man Pastor had stuttered. When he became a Christian, he longed to be a pastor, but his faltering speech seemed too big a barrier. Nevertheless, he enrolled in bible college, praying for a miracle. His speech was so poor, he was even exempted from making oral presentations. One Sunday the congregation laid hands on him in church. Pastor left the service dancing and praising God without a trip of foot or tongue. He always took this healing as a sign of his calling and an example of what the Lord had done in his life.

"Saamo says that he is worse than a heathen now. Her people came to talk to him, but he wouldn't listen and chased them away. What happens," Mary wondered again, "to change someone so much?"

I shook my head, overwhelmed. I was out of my depth.

"Saamo wanted to know if Pastor had claimed that she wasn't respectful of him. She said that is often the charge brought against a wife you want to be rid of."

"Did he?"

"No. He could hardly do that. He's complained to me so many times about other men who have used it as an excuse. Once he told me of a man who had even said that his wife was beating him. Pastor said that the man's wife had had twins. The man was frightened and wanted to send her away. I even remember exactly what Pastor said then. He said . . ." Mary stopped. She started again with difficulty. "He said, 'I thank God for Christ. Only he can save me from such fear.' "

With an uncharacteristic gesture, she bent her head, and for a moment my sense of tragedy was so great I thought she had broken.

When she spoke again, I could barely hear her. "I have not prayed enough."

"Oh, Mary." I was crying. "One more prayer would not have made anything better."

She was silent for a long time. Then she straightened. "I am glad that you have been here during this time. It has made it easier."

Her unexpected kindness undid me. I fumbled into a response. "I'm so glad I could be here for you."

But I had misunderstood her, or she retreated from what she had meant. "Because you were here," she explained, "people have been more hesitant about coming and spilling everything out. I think that is best."

I nodded, bowing to her rendition.

"The puzzling thing," she said slowly, "is that the one issue I thought was really relevant seems to be the least important."

"What's that?"

"Saamo's barrenness."

Those two words unlocked a door that then swung free in my mind. I walked out into a landscape of understanding. I saw Pastor turning in slow motion, as if trapped in stagnant water, and asking about the petrol. He seemed to shrink, his image reflected as bent in Mary's round glasses. The helpless movement he made with his hands spoke to me of both his life works slipping away—the sons essential to a man's quiver dying in the false contractions of a fit and the vision of a transforming word miscarried his manhood spent among childless women.

I saw Saamo standing alone with her hand splayed across her belly, looking across the dead fields. She was a woman isolated by her tribal background, lacking the sisterly wives that speed women's eternal tasks, her firm breasts proof of her fruitlessness, her female body a fatal trap, a sealed fountain.

I saw Mary caught out on the red-as-a-wound dirt road that slashed through the encircling compounds, her hands hanging open at her sides, her face foreign in its every contour, as she watched Pastor—her equal, her partner, her source—simply walk away.

And then, finally, I saw myself. Mary's opaqueness and aloneness had fascinated me. Her reticence had lured me on into her life, a gauche, inexperienced hunter, not sure what it was that led me to pursue something I did not even know the shape of. Too young to be familiar with either the married or the single state, too young to know anything about a life's work or what it takes to spend twenty years as a stranger in a strange land, I had blundered by landmarks in Mary's life as large as trees as if they were nothing and had stopped to ponder the unconsidered gesture of a moment as if it revealed worlds of truth. I was lost in the pursuit of the impetus of her life, expecting it to stand out and stop still, grand and succinct, complete and tangible. I wanted to capture her and put her on my wall at home, where I vainly hoped she would guide me with blank, glassed gaze and motionless nostrils. I had looked into Mary's eyes, sure that her reason for living was there to be seen, and, of course, it was not but, like everything else about her, was veiled and hidden.

Mary was wrong. Barrenness had everything to do with us: those dead in the water.

The next day Mary drove me to the Nalerigu lorry park. I was returning to Tamale by public transportation since Mary had to stay to work on the translation.

The lorry park was a large dirt field in the middle of town with abandoned trucks littering its edges. Women on small stools cooked over open fires as men talked in groups beneath the trees that ringed the park.

Mary had parked under a mango tree. I leaned my head against the hard seat and watched red ants scurry up the trunk until they were hidden by the green leaves.

"So," I said wearily, my eyes closed. "Now what?"

Mary did not ask what I meant. "The pastor in Fituu has occasionally helped me with the translating. I shall probably move there to work with him."

"And Saamo?"

"She will be returning to her people."

"She is leaving him."

"Yes."

"And what about . . ." I stopped. Bijabo. Ninkpo. Bat-

98

bik. Pastor. The list was too long. I did not want to know. And Mary did not ask who I meant.

We were silent. Nearby, a huge man stripped to the waist split wood with a fluid motion. Sweat translated his skin to the slick purple of eggplant. Although tiring, he performed the work with smooth regularity. He heaved the mighty mallet upward, and, at the height of his swing, the mallet seemed weightless, his muscles neither pushing nor pulling. Mallet and body and sky equal forces. For once, all laws suspended. Then his hands plunged down, pulled by the mallet's weight, pushed by the sky, shattering the wood, and reverberating with a jolt.

On the far side of the park appeared a rickety Mercedes-Benz bus. Across its top, round as a child's forehead, was the slogan SEA NEVER DRY. The bus trundled in and choked to a halt. Even before it stopped rolling, hundreds of people had converged on it.

Mary and I got out of the truck to view the fray. Already far more people pressed around the bus than would ever fit inside. How would I get on? The next bus wouldn't arrive until the next day, and I had work to do in Tamale.

That morning, Ninkpo had offered some reassurance when he heard that I was to take public transportation. "Don't worry," he said. "The driver will pity you because you whites cannot struggle like we can."

I decided to push forward, however, and try my luck. Grasping my shoulder strap, I put a hand on the first shoulder I came to and asked to be excused. I managed to get halfway through the crowd this way. Then I came to a halt. I would get no farther: the people ahead of me had a chance of boarding the bus and were standing fast. I twisted to see if I could see Mary, but I could not. When I turned back, the smiling ticket seller had barged through the crowd to ask if I would like a ticket.

About twice as many people as the bus was designed

to carry boarded it. A conservative estimate would put the number inside at one hundred and thirty adults. This count would not include one child per woman, one bag per person, countless chickens, a bedroll, a bunch of pots and pans, and two huge truck batteries. Four of us sat in a two-person seat near the back door.

Mary approached my window to say good-bye. I angled my hand out to grasp hers. It was dry and hard. "Thanks," I said, straining to catch a glimpse of her. She nodded. I clutched her hand longer than courtesy required. I searched for comforting words but found none and then wondered if I had been hoping she would comfort me.

The bus rumbled to life, and I let go of her hand. I gave her a cheerful wave, the kind I've seen given from toy trains. Mary stood silent, straight, her arms at her sides. We left the park, and I saw her no more.

As the bus picked up speed, the driver honked at the goats that darted into his path, wrenching the wheel to dodge them. We were so packed that none of us went sprawling.

We reached the outskirts of Nalerigu and the land stretched away, interrupted here and there by scrub trees and low, broken hills. In the distance, a cluster of compounds rose like rocks from the ground, and beyond them brooded the low gray smoke of a bush-clearing fire. The sky was a molten mirror. I thought of Dosau as it had been that morning: the bristling thatch, the pebbled walls, the closed wooden shutters, the thin paths meandering between compounds, an old man in a dark doorway wearing a white hat.

Now, as I remember those images, I search for some intimation of what was to come, a harbinger, a warning of any kind. Had there been a man sitting under a tree, a figure lurking in the shadows, an open, unwatched fire?

Anything to tell me that two years later Batbik, the

chief's son, would be murdered and the village of Dosau burned to the ground?

Batbik was sitting under a tree reading his bible when the warriors came. They were from the neighboring tribe—the group whose language Mary had first translated—and had already attacked the villages around Dosau.

Most of the people of Dosau escaped, as they were perhaps intended to, but not Batbik. He stayed under his tree. The warriors had rifles and shot at him, but he was not hit. Some said that God had intervened. If so, God did not intervene a second time. The warriors pulled out their machetes and set upon Batbik and killed him. Then they set fire to the thatch of the huts, the wooden doorways and windows, and the stalls in the market. All that is left of Dosau now are the mud shells of huts.

"Batbik used to come visit me in Fituu," Mary wrote, her handwriting large and unsteady. Her eyesight had worsened. "I gave him some back translation to do so he could earn a little money. On one visit, he told me how his family had now 'rejected' him, that is, they had beaten him unconscious on the orders of his father, the chief. When I heard of his murder, I wondered if God had not said to him, 'You have suffered enough.'

"Pastor's compound was burned down along with the others, and he fled to Fituu to stay with his brother. His home village, five miles from Dosau, was also burnt down, so all of his family there also fled."

But I did not know these things as we hurtled down the road, leaving the village far behind, our destinies inextricably linked by proximity. All I knew of the future was that a pall of smoke lowered as we rounded a corner, and suddenly flames arched over the road just ahead. The tall, dry grasses on both sides were burning like incendiary beacons. The flames lunged for fuel but found none above the barren road. I braced myself with horror, but our tin ship did not stop. We drove straight into the burning bush.

The windows became an opalescent swirl of gold and copper, heat flashed like strobes, and then we were out, beyond, on the other side. Shaken and uncertain, but whole.

LENT

The Arrest

It was just before noon on a Sunday several months later. Tamale lay deserted, the streets empty. Even the midtown water pump was, for once, abandoned. Only a dog slept in the shadow of a rusting blue bus.

Heat wriggled along the red road, quick as a snake. The yellowed trees lining it bowed to the reigning sun. Concrete telephone poles stood among the trees like sentries, their wires absent or impotent. Beyond them baked parched brown gardens of okra and corn.

I noted these sights idly. Mary's new, air-conditioned truck separated us from them. The interior smelled of plastic. The engine hummed. The body rode high above the road. Everything in the gray truck was padded—the ceiling, the steering wheel, the form-fitting seats. Amid such comfort it was easy to be disinterested in the world outside. The town slipped past, silent and odorless.

I let my head fall against the headrest and closed my eyes. We were within a mile of home, and I was glad. It had been a long trip, despite the comfort of the truck. Into my dreamy anticipation of a bath and lunch came the braying of a horn. The honking sounded only faintly in our self-contained world, but its insistence was clear. I opened my eyes and looked in my mirror.

It was a police Jeep. We would have to stop.

That day, Mary and I were returning from Ghana's neighboring country, Togo, where we had gone to buy Mary this new truck. Her battered pickup of a decade no longer weathered roads fit only for tractors, so she had been persuaded to buy a new truck, one with air-conditioning and kinder seats. At first, she resisted. Twenty years of spartan living spoke against it. But some truck was necessary, so why not a comfortable one?

We traveled to Togo whenever we needed Western goods. Ghana no longer imported such things as soap, toilet paper, matches, light bulbs, cloth, and vehicles. Mary could have gone alone, but I tagged along to take a vacation amid the Western pleasures of the francophone capital, Lomé.

In Ghana, those with means—the wealthy and the foreign—had fled. Those remaining had in common that none were well off. Even those with some money had nowhere to spend it and, lacking the Western symbols of affluence, appeared as impoverished as the rest. The equality of the Ghanaians, however undesired, was absolute. In Togo, however, the usual ranks of an enterprising third world country were very much in order.

Hotels with cavernous lobbies loomed over small Indian grocery stores with hand-lettered signs. Opposite a pristine swimming pool was an open field used as a latrine. In a rest room complete with marble sinks and dusky mirrors, an unwatched pot of pepper stew bubbled over a charcoal brazier.

Beggars lined the streets, crouched between the parked Mercedes-Benzes. In Ghana, the poorer of the two countries, I had not seen a beggar since arriving. Disparity, not poverty it seems, creates beggars.

At night the beggars went home, and the prostitutes came out. The switch revealed much: anyone not begging was selling something, most often the caricatures of luxury spawned by capitalism. Plastic sandals, fake ivory, unlit digital watches, garish boxes of bubble gum, and perfume bottles filled with suspicious-looking liquids. I paid the smallest of a group of boys to "guard" our borrowed car (that meant, according to common lore, not to damage it themselves), but as I got in I saw the largest boy take the money from him with a careless cuff.

These juxtapositions did not stop me from reveling in things I had not enjoyed in months. I went out every night for dinners of bread, cheese, fresh meat, and chocolate. I saw an entirely forgettable movie. I took showers. I sprawled in air-conditioned lobbies, reminding myself of temperatures below 90 degrees Fahrenheit. I ran my hand along every shiny car in the Datsun dealer's showroom and walked the aisles of a supermarket mouthing the brand names: Campbell's, Heinz, Kellogg's, Lipton.

We stayed in a simple resthouse run by a group connected to the institute. They had lent us the car we drove around town and provided meals of the local food. Each night Mary remained behind at the resthouse and ate its dinner of yams and stew. "I prefer home cooking," she told me firmly when I asked her to accompany me. And each night I went out the door shaking my head, unable to imagine not being lured. The trappings of civilization fell naturally about my body, just as if I had never abandoned their heavy folds. Shedding their weight again would not be easy.

Mary took a week to complete the paperwork required for the truck and to buy items others had requested. Just as we prepared to leave Lomé, the truck so full that Mary was utterly dependent on her outside mirror, the border between Ghana and Togo closed. Such closures were common, a political maneuver to state displeasure. To get home we would have to travel north into

Upper Volta [now known as Burkina Faso] and then cross down into Ghana. Assuming, of course, that the border between Upper Volta and Ghana had not also closed in the meantime.

We took five days to drive up through Togo, stopping in translators' homes and Catholic missions. We reached the final border the morning of the sixth day. Spread under the desert sky was a collection of low buildings resembling a military outpost. Nomadic women—wearing their wealth of amber and gold—wandered the dusty grounds selling milk from leather skins. A man in a Jeep smoked a cigarette. On the veranda of the main building, dozens of people dozed against their cloth-bound bundles.

Upper Volta was letting people out of Upper Volta, we were told, but wasn't sure if Ghana was letting them in. We wouldn't know until we got there. "Please," the Upper Voltan immigration officer warned, "if you enter you cannot come back." I pictured us adrift in the several miles of open bush that lay between the two countries, free to leave, but not to enter. Trapped. We had no choice, however, but to try to cross over.

We spent the day involved in Upper Volta's border formalities. The proceedings had rules as arcane and fixed as chess. After all these years, even Mary moved tentatively through the inefficient intricacies, using patience as her only strategy. She repeated the same facts and showed the same papers to each official we met, and each asked the same questions and claimed the same inability to judge.

As impassive face succeeded impassive face, I grew impatient. Why could no one make an independent decision? Such cases as ours were common. They should be ready for us. I folded my hands in my lap, wondering at myself. I had crossed borders before. I should be used to the rituals of African bureaucracy.

A fan spun overhead. The room was bare except for a metal filing cabinet, our chairs, and the official's huge wooden desk. On the desk lay a newspaper, folded open to the football scores, and a large black phone. No sign of papers or pens. The official rested his elbows on the desktop and his aligned forefingers against his mouth. He shook his head as Mary talked. Into my mind, unbidden, rose the image of the African doorman at one of the exclusive West German hotels in Lomé. How he sprang to open the door for me, his smile generous, his "Good morning, madam" designed to please.

I stood abruptly. Mary and the official looked at me, startled. But the conversation had reached some kind of conclusion, because Mary stood as well. She reached over the desk to shake hands with the official and repeated the name of the next official we were to see.

After several more such offices and conversations, we were taken to the local bar, where the top official held court. He sat outside, an orange umbrella tilted above his table. Final negotiations were made there. Mary's new truck was enviously inspected, and we were given permission to continue. Mary bent her head over the steering wheel before turning the ignition key.

We stopped at the one-room post centered between the two countries' borders. The appropriate official was not inside. While Mary began to search for him, I turned away. I had had enough.

I wandered over to a small market alongside the road. It was late afternoon. Most of the vendors had left, and the rest were packing their wares. As I walked between the deserted stalls, the dust settling in the slanting light, I came across a man with one item left on his wooden counter. A kente cloth. The real thing. Six whole yards of flawless black and gold, heavy as a lover's body across my arm. The vendor eyed me.

Kente cloth is among the finest woven cloth in the world. I knew: my mother had collected it. African art traders had come to spread their wares on our driveway in Accra and bargain peaceably through the morning.

The wealth of art I saw there! The wooden betrothal combs, the Ashanti stools, the gold weights, the bronze figurines, the wood carvings, the woven baskets, the glass beads, the leather bags, the painted gourds, the taut drums, the stringed instruments, even the occasional tree-sized snakeskin. The kente cloth had always been my favorite. Unfortunately, genuine kente was difficult to find now. The Ashanti—the tribe who wove the cloth—no longer had access to thread, and fewer men learned to weave.

It was doubly rare then to have seen another kente just days before. On the drive to Upper Volta, Mary and I had passed a long white ribbon unfurled across the land. We had whipped by before I realized what it was and had Mary turn back. A man was weaving kente. The angular wooden loom encircled him like a brown spider at the end of a sticky thread. The ribbon of white threads was as wide as his palm and stretched a hundred feet in front of him. He elevated the alternate threads, shot the shuttle through, raised the opposite threads, and shot the shuttle back. Each hand echoed the other.

Watching mesmerized me. His movements were rhythmic and even, polished by the stream of generations. Weaving is as ancient as art itself. Once in a loom you touch all time. The weaver's movements—taught by time— are arrested and held forever present by the medium. By weaving the conflicting currents of color and direction into smooth surfaces, in synthesizing beauty from diversity, the weaver creates a living stillness.

While the cloth strip in Togo had been lovely, it was no match for the kente now before me. This was exquisite. Each color was as rich and deep as the next, every thread of the finest quality. The strips were evenly woven and neatly sewn together, and the pattern the weaver had chosen was deceptively simple, as if he luxuriated in complexities regardless of their result. The work of a master.

"How much?" I asked, scarcely daring, feeling the question sacrilegious.

The vendor looked away. He was an aspiring man, to judge from the flair of his clothing. He had a low hairline, wide nose, and lips round and parted like the sections of an orange. He was reluctant, I realized suddenly. Not with the usual bargainer's feigned indifference, but genuinely. He did not want to sell the cloth.

"Dollars?"

"I have only CFA," I replied. This was the francophone currency of Africa and, while more stable than the Ghanaian cedi, it was not as valuable as the American dollar.

He named a price equal to one hundred dollars. Most would not have blinked at four times the price. I grimaced. I had only thirty dollars' worth of CFA left. I told him so.

He regarded me for the first time, glancing back and forth between my eyes. His were tinged amber, the lingering sign of some illness. He broke our gaze to stare at his square hands and then ran one along the dense, silky cloth. He seemed afraid that he or it would awaken. His nostrils flared.

"I will take it."

I ran back to the truck to get the money. Mary had been searching for me and was anxious to leave. We might not reach the border before it closed for the night. But, when pressed, she let me return to buy the cloth.

I held the money out to the vendor, but he did not lift his hand. Uncertainly, I laid the bills on the table. An evening breeze lifted them like fluff and would have whisked them away had I not extended a hand. Their paper ends fluttered beside the ample curves of the folded kente, and then stilled. The vendor did not move. I gathered the bulky cloth into my hands, lifting its sun-warmed folds as I would a child.

He raised his eyebrows when I breathed some compliment, but his gaze did not leave the cloth. The wooden frame of the stall threw a shadow across his face. The

111

light limned instead the heavy folds in my hands, the gold gleaming like jewelry against the skin-smooth black.

Turning, I walked away like a thief who expects the recalling shout with each step. With an effort, I prevented myself from running.

In the truck, I thrust aside several boxes of tinned cocoa, pressed the cloth beneath them, and pushed the goods back on top. I would have to guard against losing this treasure. Only when we were safely on the road did I start to relax.

As Mary accelerated, I felt a rush of pleasure. The kente cloth was mine! Africa's purest expression. The certainty of possession soothed away the indignities of the day. I was back in control, as I had been in Lomé.

The Ghana side of the border was closing for the evening just as we reached it. In the dusk several soldiers dragged a metal barrier across the dusty road. They seemed huge in their inappropriate rain-forest-green fatigues and bulbous boots. Mary's expression was close to reproach. She nodded at the glove compartment, and I opened it to retrieve some bars of Camay soap. Someone had pressed them on her in Lomé. "Just in case," he had said.

I bit my lip. I had had to buy that cloth. Why was it that every time I was with Mary something went wrong? I felt caught in an endless performance of fumbled lines.

Several months before, when I had returned from my trip to Dosau, the institute director's wife, Carol, had asked me how the visit with Mary had gone.

"It went well," I said, and paused, searching for a brief phrase that might capture some of the less extraordinary aspects of that trip.

She nodded, then spoke thoughtfully. "It meant a lot to her that you wanted to visit."

When I, embarrassed, shrugged this comment off, she continued, pressing the point home. She mentioned that I had been unable to travel to Dosau the first time

Mary and I had planned because of an illness. "When you couldn't go with her," Carol added, "she was really disappointed. She cried."

I stared at her. "I don't think so."

"Oh, yes."

I looked away, appalled that Mary might have depended on me. I could hardly have lived up to any expectation Mary had, what with my incessant questions and awkward comforting. Surely Carol had misunderstood. Moments later, I had already dismissed the idea.

Then, a month after my conversation with Carol and the day after Mary returned from Dosau, I was starting north on another trip. Mary and I met in the institute's resthouse, where I had gone to collect a cooler and some groceries.

Mary was cooking in the kitchen. I came upon her stirring batter in a bowl, her elbow up, the muscles of her forearm corded. Neatly rolled curlers lay in rows under her scarf. Behind her the mosquito-screened window splintered the green and gold of a mango tree into the dabs of an Impressionist's brush. Through its slender burglarproof bars stole a dusty light. I had not seen Mary since our difficult time together in Dosau, and something about her domesticity and the light caught at my throat.

My greeting was warm. She nodded and smiled but was reserved, her attention on the bowl. I grew unsure. Casting about for a topic, I asked her about Pastor and Saamo.

Things had not improved, Mary answered. Since Bijabo had gone back to his secondary school, Saamo had felt free to leave Dosau and go to her family. She would probably not return. She was planning to use her new teaching skills to find a job. She might adopt a daughter, an idea Pastor had vetoed when she had suggested it before.

I nodded and made some comment. Mary continued to stir. Perhaps she was not interested in a long conversation. While puzzled by her lack of response, I turned and was about to leave when she spoke.

"I hear you've been on your own this last week," she said with a smile. She referred to the absence of my three Tamale housemates, all schoolteachers.

Reassured, I leaned against the doorjamb. She wasn't shutting me out: it was only that, like me, she found it difficult to converse.

"Yeah," I responded. "Ginia and Mary are teaching in the villages, and Melody just returned from Bolgatanga. I had the house to myself."

"How did you like it, being all alone?" she asked. Her attention, focused on the bowl, drew my eyes along with hers. Staring at her strong hands, I answered absently.

"It was great. The house was quiet. I could spread my writing out on the kitchen table. I could get up when I wanted to. At night I could read and no one bothered me." This was true. I enjoyed being alone. But I did not tell her of the times when I had woken late at night, frightened, some allusive sound scrabbling along the edges of my dulled mind. By the time I had lifted my eyes to hers, it was too late to add these comments. A faint color rose in her cheeks.

Tragedy. The word bloomed in my mind. For a moment, I was like an actor who, her heart skipping a beat, utters the words that cause the fateful machinery of the play to lurch into motion.

Mary looked back at her bowl. "It is nice for a while," she murmured, the moment passing. But I knew we couldn't go back. The rest of our play must be faltered through, the outcome known, unbearable.

At the Ghana border, I handed the bars of soap to Mary. A soldier left the barrier to approach the truck, indicating with his hands that we should turn around. And go where? I thought. The Lomé border would have closed by now,

114

and we couldn't sleep in the full truck. Nothing resembling a house lay in the uncultivated bush between the borders. And while we could sleep outside, we had nothing to sleep upon. No, we had to get through.

The soldier came to Mary's window, gruff but expectant, and she handed out the soap. Her matter-of-factness about doing something she hated made me feel smaller.

Grudgingly, the soldiers tugged the gate open just enough to let us through. The exhausted official inside completed our papers by kerosene light. After the usual complications, we were allowed in. We spent the night in a Catholic mission, and early the next morning—before they served breakfast—we started the last leg of our journey.

And so it was that I came to that road in Tamale just a mile from home where the police Jeep appeared honking behind us—tired, hungry, made insular by satiation.

Mary slowed and bumped over the edge of the road, rolling to a stop on the dirt shoulder. She rolled down her window, and warmth rushed over us. The heat had silenced the birds but not the whir of insects. The acrid smell of stirred-up dust and exhaust drifted in.

The rusty Jeep sped past us, cut into our path, and stalled to an abrupt halt. A young man leapt out of the Jeep and ran over to us. A gun was slung carelessly at his waist, but he wore no uniform. His rumpled clothing hung askew on his body; his shirt was half tucked.

He spoke without preamble. "Why aren't you having a license plate?" he asked belligerently. He surveyed the truck, taking in the treaded tires, smooth sides, and unscratched paint.

Mary pulled out her sheaf of papers. "We arrived at the border late last night," she explained. "The official there hadn't time to fill out the temporary license plate forms. He gave me a waiver and told me to go to the immigration office first thing Monday morning. He said I could get the plates there."

The young man was impatient with her explanation. "It is illegal. You cannot drive without a license plate."

I tightened my hand on my seat belt.

Mary tugged the waiver out from among the other papers. "He told me that if I got the plates Monday morning it would be soon enough."

He repeated, his voice rising, "It is illegal. You aren't having a license plate."

"Oh, please!" I muttered, exasperated. He looked at me.

Mary angled the waiver in the window so they could both read it. He grasped one end. As she started her explanation again, her voice louder for emphasis, he tried to pull the paper from her hands. Ostensibly, he wanted to see it more clearly, but his eyes did not linger on the page. The paper was Mary's only proof of her legal status. Without it, her situation would be grave. Mary did not let go.

"Give this paper to me," he said, bridling.

Mary responded in kind. "But, you're not even in uniform. How do I know that you're really a policeman?"

The unnatural gray-blue of the truck's interior framed his face as he registered this direct affront. The trees on the opposite side of the road rustled in a sudden breeze that brought with it the close smell of his sweat.

"Do you . . ." Anger impeded his search for words. "Do you think you are in Britain, where you can do as you please? That you can just drive any way? I'm telling you, you cannot abuse me as if I was some small boy!"

The sunlight overhead threw his face into relief. It caught on the uneven texture of his skin and the bristles of his mustache. A vein in the hollow of his temple pulsed next to the rounded lids of his eyes.

Mary lifted the waiver again, and he slapped it with the back of his hand. "You are under arrest," he barked, straightening his shoulders. "You have disobeyed myself, who am a police officer, and the law. Follow me to the police station." He stalked back to his Jeep, jumped in, wheeled in reverse, and screeched off.

He must be joking, I thought. Obviously Mary did not think so. Her face had paled with apprehension. As Mary started the truck, I rubbed my hand along the plush seat beside my thigh. Arrest us for lacking a license plate! This was nonsense. How could he be serious? No Ghanaian would keep a white person under arrest for long. I thought of the African doorman.

The police station was just three blocks from where we had been stopped. Every Sunday on the way to church we walked past it. The old British building had thick walls and a deep veranda that faced Tamale's military parade ground. The road to the station reached a dead end at the fence of trees separating the station from the parade ground. A group of men lounged on the steps of the veranda and under the shade tree out front. None of them was in uniform.

The young man was standing, talking to them. He grew more animated when he saw our truck arrive and said something that made them laugh. He turned, pleased, and lifted his hand in our direction as if we were a prize. They laughed again. The young man strode toward us, his smile fading. He opened my door with a scowl.

I looked bitterly at the laughing men. No deference was to be shown here. They thought it amusing to arrest us on some specious charge. Well, I thought, I wasn't powerless. It was time this game stopped.

Stepping down from the truck, I kept my hand on the padded handle inside the door. "I would like to know," I said coldly, "if Mr. Quarshie is here. He is a friend of mine and I would like to speak to him." Mr. Quarshie was the chief of police. Actually, he was the friend of one of my housemates, but he would remember me.

For a moment I thought the young man would spit

in my face. I shrank back against the truck, my defiance gone. His eyes wide open, his jaw rigid, he leaned toward me.

"You *white* people," he spat.

I averted my face as if I had been hit. I had never been spoken to with such contempt. This is no game, I thought with sudden terror. This is for real.

I abruptly came to my senses. I had been behaving as an American, assuming I had control where I had none. I had seen the gun at his hip as a sign of authority, instead of as a weapon. I had assumed that there was a hierarchy, that he was responsible to others, when no others were in sight. How could I have misjudged things so badly?

He slashed upward with his open hand, and I jerked my face away. "You think to make a fool of me," he taunted. "You think you can just walk in here and be served tea. You think you can call anyone and they will save you." He leaned forward again, his breath full on my tilted face, speaking each word with heavy emphasis. "It is not that way here."

I did not stir; his breathing labored near my ear. Then he broke our tableau. He grabbed my arm and pulled me. toward the veranda. I tripped and grasped for the stability of the truck, but it was out of reach. The pressure of his fingers kept me upright.

Once on the veranda, the young man stopped. Mary had followed us, her face watchful. I stood awkwardly, trying not to angle my body away from him. His fingers tightened to keep a grip despite our sweat. The pale flesh of my arm bulged between the spread of his dark fingers.

The group of men had returned to their conversation. The twelve lounged on the veranda steps and low wooden chairs. One leaned against a tree, scrubbing his teeth with a stick. They were young—slim city boys, not farmers—and dressed in dark Western clothes. They had sat all morning and would sit all afternoon.

The young man turned to the group and pursed his lips. Abruptly, he bellowed something in the vernacular, then laughed. The men smiled, but their glance slid over us and they continued their discussion.

The young man hunched a shoulder back. His attention flickered to us, then back to the men. The men ignored him. He flung my arm away and launched into pacing. Grains of the eroding concrete floor grated under his heel.

He whipped out of his second turn shouting at us. "You think you are better than we blacks!" Watching the men—whose attention he had regained—out of the corner of his eye, he shook a fist. "It is not enough to you to rob this our country, to spoil it, when we, in fact, were too weak to defend. It is not enough to you."

Mary started to speak, but this fueled his fury. "You must also abuse me," he thundered. "You are making me to be a fool, but I am no fool!"

"I do not believe you to be a fool," Mary said quietly. "I think we have just had a misunderstanding. These papers show that I am not . . ."

He interrupted. "You think you can do as you please, you whites. Nothing can stand in your way. Well, I am here in your way. And we will see who will treat who. We will see."

The young man resumed pacing. Two doors opened off the veranda into the station. A man sat inside at a desk. On noticing this, Mary nodded at the young man and turned to walk into the building. I followed, not wanting to be left alone.

The young man strutted after us, jeering. "Go! See if he can save you. He cannot!"

Light filtered through the slats of a wooden shutter behind the desk. The overhead fan wobbled round and round, squeaking at the same point in each journey. The dingy white walls had darkened at shoulder level from leaning bodies.

119

Behind the elevated desk, a man slept with his head on his folded arms. He was an older man, the only one wearing a police uniform, although it would not survive many more washings. Next to him a man stretched out asleep on a chair, his head back against the wall. Apparently, disturbances were not common on Sunday afternoons.

Mary spoke a word to the older man, who awoke. He sat on a platform behind the desk so that even though Mary stood, they were eye to eye. Mary began to explain the papers once again.

The officer nodded but leaned back in his chair to glimpse the young man shouting. His eyes returned to Mary's face, and he nodded again, but he seemed to be listening to the young man. When she finished, he smiled and said, "I am sorry. There is nothing I can do. It is illegal to drive without a license plate."

"Yes, I know," Mary replied, her patience starting to fray. "But I could not have had one. We arrived in Ghana after dark yesterday and today is Sunday and nothing is open. How could I have gotten this license plate?"

He shrugged. "I don't know." He nodded in the direction of the young man's voice. "Anyhow, he will decide what to do."

The young man's shouting had not abated. If anything, he was becoming louder. When he stalked past the doorway, his palm rested on the butt of his gun. I did not want to think about what kind of decision we could expect from him.

I studied the police officer's face: had he no qualms about abandoning us to this man? The officer smiled—the only defense of the powerless—and nodded to confirm his remarks. I looked over at Mary. What did she think? Mary had pulled off her glasses and was wiping them deliberately. Without them she looked frail, the bridge of her nose pinched red. So far, I had been less helpful to her than either man.

She replaced her glasses, and we returned to the veranda. After a moment's hesitation, we sat on a bench propped against the wall. I nervously fingered the metallic coolness of a nail poking from the bench. The young man was standing on the edge of the veranda, staring at the truck. He turned, his body enlarging as he advanced.

He switched to English. "You take me for a fool. But I am knowing you. You think because you are white that you own me. That you can wave your hand there and I will go or you can wave your hand here and I will come. You cannot abuse me."

He glared at us, cracked his neck with a swift motion, and returned to pacing. Mary used the silence to respond. "It appears that an error has been made," she acknowledged. "I agree that this is so." She paused. "I would like to ask a favor, though." She paused again, and when he did not say anything, continued. "Would you allow us to take the vehicle to our office and unload it?"

Mary was concerned that the vehicle and its small fortune in Togolese goods would be appropriated. A friend of ours in Accra had imported and paid for a car which was then taken by the government. He never saw a pesewa for it but often saw the car being driven by soldiers.

"Eh!" the young man said, turning with astonishment to his fellows. "First they make me to be a fool and now they take me for a thief." He bent toward us, and I drew back against the wall. "What insult is coming next?" he snarled. Straightening, he walked over to the men.

"Nothing will move until I decide," he declared over his shoulder, squatting to speak to the men.

His attention off us for the first time, I felt free to focus on him. None of this was necessary for a simple arrest. Why didn't he do something? Why weren't we filling out some sort of paper? How long would we just sit here? What kind of arrest was this, anyway? Then he turned his head, his eyes narrowing with menace, and I looked away, cowed. Bunching my skirt in a damp hand, I tried to maintain composure.

My gaze skimmed the veranda, the men, the trees of the yard, and came to rest on the truck. It was parked at an angle—blunt, gray, smooth, a ship stilled. Amid the rough concrete buildings and dirt road, it seemed as mysterious as an icon, the mirrors of its shiny sides absorbing nothing, reflecting all. Along with the African light it rejected, to me returned other reflections.

I was in high school in Seattle. A black girlfriend and I had gone downtown to the police station to observe a hearing for class. We were leaving, waiting in the silent lobby for an elevator, when two white police officers and a black man careened by. The police each clenched one of the man's arms. He was struggling. They collided with an ashtray stand, which slammed into the wall with a metallic report and shot sand across the carpet. The elevator door slid open, and the three of them crashed in, hitting the back wall with a brutal thud. As the door whispered shut, the two white men inched the still struggling black man to the floor.

I stood in shock, and Bonnie began to cry. I murmured something ineffectual, and she turned on me. "You don't understand!" she accused. "He'll never get out of here. They'll take him up there and he'll never get out." I stared at her, taken aback. But there's no permanent jail in this building, I was about to protest. I didn't say it though. Suddenly I knew what she meant, how deep things ran. And when the metal door slithered open again, ready to take us down, I hesitated before stepping over its threshold.

The truck's glare shifted as I shifted on the bench, returning to me a different reflection. At the airport in

Rome, coming through a checkpoint to catch my flight to Ghana, I noticed the man behind me. At four in the morning, he and I were the only ones about, except for the airport guards. He was African, to guess from his deep color, and dressed urbanely. As I reached for the strap of my shoulder bag, some of the security guards slipped from behind the metal-detecting machine and sauntered up to him. I stopped to watch.

The six of them smiled as men do who are anticipating sport. The African smiled uncertainly as they surrounded him. The guards asked something in Italian, but he shook his head. He responded in German, then French, and then admitted in English that he did not speak Italian. His accent was British. As he spoke, he kept changing his grip on his bag.

The guards smiled at each other, and one motioned for him to hand over the bag. He did so with reluctance. I should go over there and say something, I thought. Perhaps my white female voice would be of help. Perhaps any voice would be of help. But what if they turned on me? I hadn't much time to catch my flight.

The African's gaze was fixed on his bag. He did not look in my direction. Perhaps he did not want my help, I thought with sudden relief. I wouldn't want to be condescending. Besides, what could the guards do, really? This was a civilized country. I hesitated and then shouldered my bag. Walking on, I glanced back. They were rifling his bag. Their frames towered over his; the metal detector a dark backdrop. My step faltered, but already my head had swung back to make sure I didn't trip. And then it was easier simply to keep walking.

The truck's dazzle dimmed as the trees rippled in a sudden breeze, changing the reflection once again. On my first trip north of Tamale, I went with Mohammed, a Ghanaian who had recently traveled to the United States. Mohammed and I rode in the front seat of the car and

123

three of his relatives in back. He drove. We shared impressions of America, and Mohammed's nephew asked us if the prejudice in the United States was as bad as was often said.

"Let me tell you a story," I responded. "One of my professors is black, middle-aged, a handsome man. The college I attend is located in a small town in the north of the country. One day this professor went to the bank, the bank he had been going to for years. Someone had left her purse on the counter—a metallic handbag. 'Of course,' said the professor's wife, who told me this story, 'he didn't pick the purse up. You learn that much as a black in this country.' "

Intent on my word choice, I turned only occasionally to Mohammed and not at all to those in the back. I attended alone to the story.

"So the professor went up to one of the bank tellers to point out the purse. Because she had turned around to check something, he touched her arm to get her attention. He knew the teller, and the bank that Friday afternoon was full. But when she turned and saw him—or shall I say his skin?—she screamed." I shook my head. "Can you believe it?" I asked, turning to look at the three Ghanaians in the backseat.

Mohammed's nephew was staring at me in horror, his whole body braced away from me as if he felt the car were about to crash. For the first time, I truly saw the story. I had told it as a fable about how ridiculous people could be, how crippling their prejudices. He had seen that in the United States any black man could be treated as a monster.

The truck's reflections—mirages of itself—were broken when I glanced sideways at Mary. She sat with her feet together, back straight, hands folded. Her stillness had something African about it. If only I could be like her, I thought.

124

Just then the man leaning against the tree—the one who had been scrubbing his teeth with a stick—said something quiet to the young man and nodded toward us. The other men stopped talking and looked away, pretending disinterest. The young man denounced the speaker loudly, but the others remained silent. The young man jumped up and paced once, caged. Then he announced in English, "It is time to take these white women to the top men." He hitched his pants with a forearm. "They will know how to deal with white people who abuse the law."

At last, I thought, my hope reviving. Others were sure to have more sense.

The young man spoke, and four of the men got up. One turned to the side and spat. They escorted us to the police Jeep, which the seven of us barely managed to fit inside of. The young man ground the gears, shot into reverse, thrust into first, and we sped off.

He first drove to a house he claimed belonged to an assistant of the chief of police. The assistant was not there. The young man drove to another officer's house, but he was not there either. He did not mention going to Mr. Quarshie's house, and neither did I. He seemed unsurprised when he found the men were not at home. Perhaps he knew they would not be.

We shot off down the street again, back to the station, he said, but before we got there he yelled a greeting to a man on the street. He hurtled off the road, halted in front of an apartment building, and jumped out. Laughing, he threw his arm around the man and strode away without a backward glance.

We sat cramped in the Jeep, not speaking, avoiding each other's gaze. No one moved. Dust settled on the grimy windshield and the mud-spackled hood. A large tree shading the Jeep dropped nuts on the hood, which hit like gunshots. I stared out my window. What if he didn't return?

About fifteen minutes later, the young man came

bounding back and drove to the police station without incident or explanation.

We returned to our respective positions, Mary and I to our bench and he to the group on the steps. He no longer shouted so much but sat thinking up things to say and shouting them when they came to him, which was less and less often. The conversation among the men had turned desultory, and several slept.

The longer nothing happened, the more trapped I felt. I scanned our setting—the young man on the steps, the truck in the sun, us on the veranda between them—and its rigidity terrified me. How would we ever get out of this stalemate? The concrete floor spread smoothly from us like a quicksand sea.

I looked for the man who had defended us, but he was gone. There was no way I could contact anyone I knew. We were helpless. The young man stirred restlessly, as if he felt trapped, too. A dangerous sign. What would he do to break out?

I waved a fly from my face and thought: Here, in the dead of a Sunday afternoon, anything could happen. Who would ever know exactly what? An unfortunate accident, they would say, and who would know better? I've got to do something, I thought. I can't just sit here, waiting for God knows what.

Mary turned to me at that moment and asked me if I would like to pray. Prayer had been the furthest thing from my mind. I nodded, and she bowed her head.

"Give us strength, Lord. Work this situation for your glory. We feel blessed to be a part of the working out of your perfect plan. We know that where we see only confusion you are there working. Keep us calm and patient and sure of you. Amen."

Then Mary put her hand to her face and started to cry.

I felt like someone had punched me. I leapt up, and only when I had reached the edge of the veranda did I realize that I was crying, too. I spoke fiercely to control my voice.

"Perhaps you *are* a fool," I hissed at the young man. "Do you know this woman? Who she is? This woman has given her *life* to your country."

Mary spoke harshly. "Be quiet!"

Now that they were out, the words seemed childish, asking for a pity I did not want. But I continued, too caught up to stop.

"This is how you repay her kindness, eh? Someone spends twenty years and it's for nothing. She can be treated like dirt by any khaki boy who thinks he is a man because he has a gun."

There was a surprised silence, whether because of my fervor or my words I do not know.

"If you cannot respect her for what she has done, you can at least respect her for being your elder."

The silence continued, and I became emboldened. I turned to Mary. "I'm leaving."

A rustle came from behind. I raised my voice. "I'm going to the house of the director of the institute. It's nearby, and he can help us out of this mess." Dean would be at church, but he would return soon. I could wait. Both his house and mine were right next to the office, and less than a mile away. I reasoned that the young man might let me go because the truck was not my vehicle. Regardless, I would not sit here a second longer.

I walked to the edge of the veranda, jumped down, and started up the road. Shouts came from behind, but I moved steadily away. Concrete-block houses shaded the road, and I put my hand out to touch a metal rainspout. Please, I prayed, and the pound of my heart fluttered into the air when a bird sang an arpeggio ending with a suspended, breathless note.

The Jeep started up and came roaring after me. I stopped and turned. The young man drove straight for

127

me. I wanted to call his bluff but retreated onto the steps of a house. He braked to a halt just a foot away and leapt out. A quick glance around me revealed what I had feared: no one was within sight or hearing.

The young man stood poised over me, hands on hips, breathing hard. I looked him in the eye, hovering between deference and defiance. Sweat ran down his furrowed brow. Then he looked down and pulled his gun. I stopped breathing. This is it, I thought. The end.

He laid the gun across his palm, his finger on the trigger. The gun was battered, the erect barrel veined with dust, the handle smudged with prints. His index finger trembled ever so slightly against the curve of metal.

I looked up to find his gaze on me. His pupils reflected my face. Pulling his finger loose, the young man tapped the gun.

"Guns," he whispered, "make all men."

Then I was back in the Jeep, gasping for breath, my limbs tingling as we whirled to race back to the police station. The young man dragged me without resistance to the bench on the veranda and pushed me onto it. Mary turned away. I gave up.

Despite my efforts, however, we were not to rot on that veranda. The men kept staring at Mary. She sat there silent, straight, her eyes fixed above their heads. Something had to be done about her. Several of the men muttered suggestions to the young man. He would respond with halfhearted heat, and they would shrug. After a little silence, they would mutter something else.

Finally, the young man rose. "It is time to go see Mr. Quarshie." At last, I thought.

Unfortunately, Mr. Quarshie was not at home. The young man let the screen door of Mr. Quarshie's house slam shut as he swaggered back toward us. I slumped in my seat.

But next door, it turned out, lived another important

police officer. The young man took us over to meet him. A boy answered our knock, and, after a short wait, a patrician man came out wearing his morning robe. He rubbed his head with the palm of his hand and smiled. He asked Mary to repeat her story, which she did. Then the young man spoke to him in Twi, explaining the situation with reserved gestures. The anger we had seen was gone.

The officer nodded and frowned. He turned to Mary and gave her an apologetic smile. "I'm terribly sorry. Not having a license plate is quite a problem. I'm afraid we must continue to keep you under arrest."

Mary put a hand to her face. The officer reached for her elbow, concerned. My God, I thought, when was this going to end? Were they actually going to take us to jail?

Mary lowered her hand. "I have spoken to this man," she enunciated, nodding at the young man, "about letting us take the vehicle and its goods to our office. If you would allow us to do this, I would be grateful."

The officer gestured angrily at the young man. "Of course," he agreed. "This should have been done before."

It came to me then. With the last of my strength, I spoke. "The office gates will be locked," I said. Mary turned to me apprehensively. "We will have to go to the Baptist Church to fetch the key from the director."

They looked at Mary, and, after a deep breath, she nodded. It was true. One parking lot had locked gates to protect such things as fully loaded vehicles. The director, Dean, was one of several people with a key. The senior officer agreed to let us go and then shook Mary's hand respectfully. The seven of us climbed back into the Jeep and drove to the Baptist Church, a large pink building. The young man parked in the alley out front.

The sound of rhythmic singing poured from the church. A woman stood in the doorway, rocking her baby and fanning herself. I was getting out of the Jeep when the young man grabbed my arm.

He leaned toward me, his grip painful. "Ask for the key," he said. "That's all. Understand?" I nodded, and he let go of my arm. "Come quickly," he added.

I pushed into the cool church—which seemed a whirl of color and movement after the deserted streets—and forward to the pew where I knew the director always sat. Fans spun above the orange and purple walls. The choir, dressed in blue robes and white handkerchiefs, sang with full, unleashed voices. The sways of the congregation were so synchronized as to appear connected by more than the tenuous threads of sound.

I reached across the others in the director's pew and tugged on his sleeve. "Hi. Can I have the keys to the office?"

His smile of pleasure at seeing me back from the trip faded to a puzzled look. "Are you all right?" he said as he dug in his pocket for the keys, his eyes on my face.

"You had better come outside," I said. I could trust myself to say nothing further without losing control.

The director followed me to the door, examined the police Jeep, then looked at me. "What's wrong?" he asked with concern. I shook my head, still unable to speak, and walked toward the Jeep. The director gazed at Mary and the five men, who also said nothing.

"What's going on here?" he asked, approaching the Jeep.

The young man's face was a mixture of annoyance and pleasure. I had disobeyed, but not by much.

He spoke to the director. "Follow us to the police station." The director nodded, got into his car around the corner, and drove behind us.

At the police station, we gathered on the veranda steps. The group of men turned to examine the director, who was an American with hairy, powerful arms. He tilted his heavy head and squinted his blue eyes against the sun.

"So," he said, putting his hands on his hips. "What

130

seems to be the problem here?" His voice was easy, loose. He looked slowly from one man to the next and smiled.

The police officers uneasily smiled back, not sure how to approach the topic. I remained silent, still unsure of my voice.

"Everything is just *basa-basa,* eh?"

They laughed in appreciation of his use of the vernacular and relaxed at his jocular tone. The young man explained about the lack of a license plate. The director glanced at us, to confirm the story, and I nodded.

He spread his hands out and laughed, inviting their laughter. "I thought this was a big problem," he joked. "This is only a small problem."

The police officers laughed, greatly relieved. At last, someone they could deal with, someone with a sense of humor. The director smiled, the police officers smiled, the young man smiled. I did not smile.

"Well. This is such a small problem," the director said. "What do you think we can do to solve such a small problem?"

"We are feeling badly." The young man pointed at us. "We are human. We do not like to see our sisters cry. But there is nothing we can do. They have been breaking the law."

The director nodded gravely. "This is a problem. But did they not tell you about our special agreement with the government?"

"No, they did not tell me." The young man and the director smiled at each other. Trust a woman to get it wrong, I could hear them think. Never mind that Mary's explanations had fallen on deaf ears.

I crossed to sit on the veranda bench. Even being saved from this situation was humiliating. How I longed to rescue myself.

The director explained that we had a contract with the government to bring vehicles into the country and that the contract listed a grace period for obtaining license plates. He explained respectfully. The young man listened. His verbal assents came in response not to crucial points but to deferential remarks the director made. I noted this with increasing unease. Perhaps the young man had been right in his accusations. Had I thought I was better than he? Was I too used to manipulating things instead of honoring people?

By the end of the conversation, the young man had been guided into nodding and found himself agreeing to take all of us back to the senior police officer's house. There the same easy, laughing exchange occurred. No papers were traded, no proofs of identification displayed, no contracts shown. They just talked. A few minutes later, we were being driven to our office with Mary's truck, all charges dropped.

At the office, everyone got out to say good-bye. Our three vehicles were the only ones in the parking lot. A passing breeze whipped around our heads feathery ashes from the surrounding fields.

The director and the police officers exchanged smiles, handshakes, and promises to get together for beer. I watched the young man. How different he seemed. His eyes were creased thin with amusement at some joke the director was making. Had I misinterpreted everything?

Bracing one hand against Mary's truck, I extended the other. "Forgive me if I offended you." The words reverberated in my skull. What was I saying? Were they a challenge or a plea?

His eyes were unfathomable. Give me some sign, I prayed. None came. He did not move, and I dropped my unshaken hand.

The other officers and he returned to the Jeep. In the side mirror, his face was like a night ocean. He gunned the motor, laughed, and roared off.

The director turned to me and laughed, too. "My goodness," he remarked with a grin. "When I saw you walk into the church I thought you guys had murdered someone."

I gave him a labored smile. "Yeah. The whole thing was pretty ridiculous, I guess."

Mary stood in front of the truck. I wanted reassurance, but she looked away. She seemed exhausted, fragile. I felt huge next to her, oafishly strong, already able to dismiss the day's effects with a lie.

The kente, I remembered abruptly, the one I had insisted on returning to buy. But the truck was locked up like a sleek metal cage, and I dared not mention the African cloth buried inside. I would have to leave without it.

"It seems I've made a bad job of everything," I confessed slowly. I recalled Mary saying, "I prefer home cooking." How would things have ended if I had grasped that proffered lifeline? We stumble at noon as in the twilight.

Mary nodded as if forgiveness were due but not yet at hand. I stepped back. "Thanks," I said, for I know not what. The word seemed scripted.

Mary and the director returned to his car. My house was only a short walk up a path, but the institute's resthouse where Mary stayed was across town. They pulled out of the parking area, and I stood in the empty lot— their footprints in the dust around me, the sun just past its height—alone.

PASSOVER

The Dinner

Without the mediation of twilight, the day charged into night. The yellows and greens of our yard sank, defeated, to gray. The sparse lawn lost ground to a shifting study in shadow. The round trees flattened into tangled webs against the purple sky. Close to the equator, the abrupt overthrow of sun is the constant upset.

Returning from the office about a month after the arrest, I pushed into the tree branches overhanging the path and emerged in our yard. From beyond the encircling trees came the first flicker of the neighbors' lanterns and the twang of water in a metal bathtub. Our bungalow loomed darker in the darkness, an outline without detail or perspective.

Like most tropical houses, ours lay beached on top of the ground. No cool, anchoring basements here. A concrete patch on the outside wall marked where the water pipes had supposedly been repaired. The water pressure had never been high enough for us to find out.

I trudged up the few steps of our veranda and tugged

the ill-fitting screen door open. After crossing the kitchen, I came to a halt in the living room.

In the United States, houses abounded with things that gave under my touch. Permanence sustained each curve. Here, everything was spartan, hard. The walls and floor were unyielding concrete; the short curtains, dark; and the few chairs, wooden. Before the press of human life could shape an object to its own comfortable proportions, decay had crumbled it. The teeming life outside abetted this dissolution, spilling into the house and scrabbling in the corners when the lights were out.

Irritated, I ran my hand along a cabinet warped from dampness. The land was like this house, I thought. It did not retain impressions. Asphalt roads were soon overrun by jungle. Abandoned houses appeared two years later as ancient as Greek ruins. Of the sprawling, wealthy empires Africa had once spawned, there were no remnants. Governments now came and went, their passing moving little more than dinner conversations. Ghana was a place, it seemed to me that night, without a history. The newspapers bore slight truth, and nature rendered all monuments dust. Humanity was like the humidity: intrinsic, but traceless. Our days were like a shadow.

Just before returning to Ghana, I had driven across Holland with a Dutch man who had spent the first nineteen years of his life in Ghana. Our families had been friends; he was my age. Karl made the trip only as a favor to me: he did not like Holland. "The land and the people are both flat," he growled, frowning at the perfect rows of tulips. When I asked if he would like to return to Ghana, he was curt.

"There's nothing there for me."

"Nothing?" He had lived in Ghana much longer than I had.

"Am I a Ghanaian? Who would I be there?"

"You wouldn't like to just see it?" I persisted. "The market or a mango?"

138

A faint smile came to his face. "Those little red birds," he said. "Do you remember them? When they flew? Like flaming arrows." He paused, his gaze flickering to the gray sky. "When we lived in Tamale," he added, "I would walk straight out our back door and keep going. For miles. Deep into the bush." His smile faded to a frown. "Returning would be a disappointment." He gave me a warning glance. "I would rather stay at sea." Karl was a sailor, all land became for him a port that did not carry the burden of "home." Now I wondered if he had been the wiser of us. What use was there in crossing the sea? Wherever I was, I longed for somewhere else, unsure which place that was and if I had ever known.

In my bedroom, I lit a kerosene lantern. The floor and walls were bare, a bed and desk the sole furniture. The room's monastic nature was broken only by the bed's blue terry-cloth sheets, a luxury for their coolness. Opposite the closet were a shower stall and a sink, neither of which had running water. Although the water came on once a week, only the tap in the hallway worked.

Scooping a calabash of tepid water into the sink, I rested my forearms on the ceramic, dropped my head, and felt the stretch all the way down my back. I let my breath out, raised my head, and bathed my face. The water tasted rusty from lying still in our barrel. When the water drained, mosquitoes rose from the pipe like tiny stars.

A breeze swept through the netting that ran the length of the hallway. Our sleeveless shirts and cotton skirts fluttered on the clothesline. Perhaps Joseph—the assistant printer at the institute—had been right to predict rain tonight. It was the first breeze since the dry, hot season had begun in earnest. For weeks temperatures had blazed around 110 degrees.

Such heat was new to me; I had never lived so close to the desert. Sweat trickled behind my knees. Cushioned chairs pressed unbearably. Direct sunlight sowed headaches. Most peculiar of all was living in an environment hotter than my own body. When using the mirror, I always started at the sink's living warmth against my belly. To find the ceramic radiating made my own heat-induced lethargy seem more pronounced. The natural order of things was reversed: the inanimate warm and lifelike, the animate cool and lifeless. Even my urine felt cold as it passed from my body.

I found Melody, one of my three housemates, in the kitchen starting dinner. She was an American in her early thirties. Melody had taught elementary school in the United States and was trained as a reading specialist. Here she taught the institute's foreign children and provided diagnostic testing. Her presence witnessed to a surge of interest in the needs of American children overseas.

"Hi, hon," she greeted me cheerfully.

I smiled. Perhaps Melody would lighten my mood. She had told me once, "I rarely find nothing to chuckle about." I believed this. In her life, frustrations were translated into comedy. She told stories at her own expense and with a flair for exaggeration that was appreciated in a storytelling culture. Those of us who had been with her during some event soon forgot, as she did, what had actually occurred. If observers did stop her to introduce some intrusive fact, her loyal listeners waved them away, more interested in her embellishments.

Melody struck a match and bent to light the wick of a kerosene lantern. The match's glow turned her reddish hair to flame and her plump face to apricot.

"I thought tonight was our night for electricity," I commented. The two sides of Tamale alternated in receiving electricity in the evening. In the south of Ghana, electricity was cheap and constant. The huge Akosombo Dam built across the Volta River readily translated the rush of water into light. Here in the north, however, the water lay still, yielding no such transmutations. Precious gasoline—itself altered by refining—was laboriously converted to electric current at a local plant.

"It was." She shook the match out and placed the glass globe over the flame. The light clarified, turning the windows opaque, viewless, and causing the cramped room to spring into form. "Someone on the other side is having a party tonight," she explained. Melody's circle of friends—and thus information—was wide.

"That accounts for it." I flicked the switch anyway. It failed to work.

Nothing here could be depended upon. Our tiny kitchen was adapted to intermittent electricity, water, and food. The stove and refrigerator used gas. A water filter protected us from the bacteria and rust that gathered in the fifty-gallon water barrel. A one-hundred-pound bag of rice, a twenty-five-pound bag of onions, three missile-shaped bottles of gas, a dozen coffee tins filled with groundnut paste, and several stacked yams made our pantry look like a survivalist's.

"Isaac's coming for dinner tonight," Melody announced as she rummaged in the pantry, pushing aside cobwebs.

"Good," I replied, but I was thinking of the article I needed to write. I had postponed writing about Mary for months. Another day's delay would have to be added. I opened the fridge to pull out a bottle of water.

Isaac was a Ghanaian friend of ours who worked as a schoolteacher. How he survived on his salary of five hundred cedis a month was a mystery. A single yam, sufficient for only five meals, cost one hundred cedis. Isaac should have been starving, but he had a roof over his head and the compact body of an athlete. He proved one writer's maxim: "Ghana is a nation of magicians." Melody was unwilling to trust Isaac's life to magic, however, so she often invited him to dinner.

After pouring two glasses of water—which instantly

141

frosted—I set one next to Melody. I took mine and leaned against the fridge, watching as Melody prepared the meal with careless ease, her movements so different from Mary's.

"Stephen will probably come by later," Melody added, wresting the key from a corned-beef tin. Stephen was another Ghanaian friend of ours. He had a university education and worked in an office. "But not too much later. There's a curfew tonight. No one's to be on the streets after ten."

"Oh. That's right." The very idea made me restless, though I hadn't planned on going out.

I took a sip of water and rolled the cool glass across my flushed cheek and eye. Through its watery distortions, the room dissolved into marshes of darkness and light.

"Did you notice?" Melody continued. I lowered the glass to find her waving at several trays on top of the refrigerator. "Stephen brought more guinea fowl eggs this morning."

"I saw them. They must be costing him a fortune." Stephen was like the African drum played only at the fortissimo outdoor performances require. He did everything full force. "Isn't this the third morning he's brought us several dozen?"

Melody nodded. "Ever since chicken eggs went to forty cedis a dozen." This price translated at the official exchange rate to thirteen dollars. We paid the equivalent of fifteen dollars for a pineapple, ten for a few bananas, and thirty for a pound of tomatoes. Paying such prices helped us understand the position of Ghanaians.

"You really shouldn't let him give them," I admonished.

"Let him?" Melody protested. "You know Stephen! I told him this morning that it was too much, that I absolutely would not accept. He acted like I had insulted his honor. How could I refuse?"

142

"I don't know," I agreed. "But he must be going penniless."

"Not on our account."

I frowned. "What do you mean?"

"I'm standing there with all sixty eggs in my arms—calculating just how many cedis they cost and how many meals he's going to miss and how successful I would be at insisting he take them back—when he grins, and tells me, 'not to worry.' They're gifts to him."

"You're kidding!"

"No! Isn't that just like him?" She pointed her spoon at me. "To make me take them and *then* tell me?"

I laughed.

"Especially when my hands are full and I can't do anything about it. Like throw one at him." She banged her spoon against the bowl.

"Still, it is nice of him," I said. "After all, he could have used the eggs himself. He wanted you to have them."

"He wanted to give me a lecture," she accused without heat. "I bet he planned the whole scene. You should have heard. About how important it is to depend on the Lord for everything, even to the extent of trusting God to provide for your friends when they put themselves out for you."

"Good advice. Tell him it's not the American way."

"That's the thing," Melody replied seriously, her hand on her hip. "Just when I think, really, this time he's pushed me too far, he says something so true I can't be mad at him. You know?"

I nodded. I knew exactly what she meant. Stephen was exasperating the way I imagined saints to be.

Melody moved to the white enamel stove, turned up a gas burner, and lit it. At the heat, a dozen brown insects scurried out of the burner. "Ugh," she said mildly, lifting the iron skillet until they had disappeared down the side of the stove. We were inured to the sight.

"Then Stephen told me," Melody said, replacing the skillet, "that I was to be his second wife."

"Another marriage proposal!" Proposing marriage was an often encountered form of teasing women, but Melody held the record in our house. Her offers numbered in the hundreds, and the cows bid for her hand had recently escalated to six. I attributed her success to her sense of humor, but she claimed the source was her beauty—and how much of it there was. Early on, Melody had written to her father about these proposals and upon receiving his response had given a dramatic sigh of relief. "I was afraid, what with the price of beef," she declared, "that he might have married me off!"

At my exclamation, Melody gave a mock beauty pose. "So," I asked, "what did you tell him, Helen?"

"That I wanted to be his first wife, of course. No second fiddle for me. But he was quite sure. I was to be his second."

"Esther still comes first." Esther was his fiancée.

"I asked if that was it, but he wouldn't say. He just repeated that I was to be second."

For some reason, Stephen disliked speaking of Esther. This puzzled us, since we often spoke of her among ourselves. She was the most beautiful woman any of us had ever seen. Stephen's reticence about her seemed remarkable given his artesian character. He insisted on stating his opinion on any number of subjects but then would not allow us even to approach others. Esther was one of them.

Melody believed she had found an explanation when a mutual friend told her that Esther was living with Stephen. Since Esther's father had received the bride-wealth, they were considered married although they had not had their church wedding. "It is the way of their tribe," the woman told Melody, and Melody nodded, understanding. Small wonder Stephen avoided the subject. How tricky the relations across cultures are: always having to weigh how much can be misunderstood. I still wondered if we had found the true explanation. How little we really knew. Coming to an understanding here was like lighting a lantern: where the light was brightest, the shadows were darkest.

I swung away from my position against the fridge and ran a finger along the rounded edge of a louvered pane in the window. It came up dusty.

"I upset Joseph today," I announced. Joseph was the man who had predicted rain.

Melody pivoted from the stove, searching my expression. "What happened?"

I told her briefly. Every morning the office generator—which ran the printing press, computers, fans, and lights—had to be started. I was one of the few people and the only woman who had been trained to do this. When Joseph and I had arrived at the office first that morning, we had set off together to start it.

The office was set in the middle of a large field. The parking lot and a water tank were in front of the building, a fuel tank and generator in back. I followed Joseph down the dirt path to the generator, passing goats munching dry grasses outside the computer room and birds flitting among the leafless bushes along the building. Beyond the field lay scattered concrete bungalows like our own. Outside one a line of women waited to fill their water basins. The tap at that house always ran, since the house lay in a hollow.

Once inside the tin shed that housed the generator, Joseph and I stood on opposite sides of the engine. It rose like a black behemoth from the concrete floor and dripped with grease. The close room reeked of diesel fuel. At one end of the engine reared a crank used to start it like a Model T. Just before the engine caught, the crank bucked in your hands. Joseph's face, above the knobby engine and against the backdrop of tin, was a brown petal.

145

He crouched on his heels to hook the generator up, his sandals flat on the floor, the tight curls on his legs showing below the dark trousers. I watched casually as his slim hands worked, but then I became more attentive. The connection seemed wrong to me, even when I crouched to study it. I hesitated, decided not to say anything, and then eyed the engine towering beside me. Its power was lethal.

I opened my mouth to suggest Joseph let me try hooking it up, but his taciturn face—the emphatic jaw and hollow cheeks—stopped me. I suggested instead that I get Dean, the director, to check it.

Joseph straightened to his feet and would not look at me. His pose was stiff. He scrubbed the backs of his hands with a rag. I looked up at him from my knees, knowing that I had offended him but unable to think of a word to say. A fly buzzed in a corner of the shed; a truck coughed to a stop in the parking lot. Our tableau seemed fixed, timeless.

I sighed and moved the window's lever so I wouldn't see my reflection in the dark glass. "I felt badly," I told Melody. "I knew he didn't appreciate a woman questioning him, but I was afraid. Those things are dangerous. What was I to do? Just pray?"

"Did you get Dean?"

"Yeah," I replied absently. The weight of the day descended. I thought back to the arrest. I kept making the same mistakes. Small comfort that they were unavoidable.

When I had returned with Dean to the tin shed, the day's first heat shimmered around the corrugated tin like an angry sea. It pushed in waves from the roof and sides. I took a breath before plunging into the still air inside.

"So?" Melody prompted. "Had Joseph done it right?"

I gave a half laugh. "Well, you know Dean—such a Solomon. He told Joseph it looked all right to him, and

146

while pointing out what was right, disconnected and reattached it. Joseph watched closely, and it looked different to me when Dean finished, but I can't be sure. Who was he humoring—Joseph or me?" I shook my head. "At any rate, we both felt vindicated. Which is why, I suppose, Dean's the director and I'm not."

Melody returned to her skillet and lowered the gas under it. "Joseph will have forgotten tomorrow," she comforted.

Restless, I shoved myself away from the window and scooped out a bowl of rice from the burlap sack in the pantry. "How was your day?" I asked, settling on a table. I sifted the rice with my fingers to remove weevils, stones, and leaves.

"Pretty routine. Except . . . oh! I forgot! You won't believe this."

"Try me."

"I came home in a police Jeep."

"You what?" My hands halted, but the rice kept slipping through my fingers.

"You heard me. The neighbors stared. It confirmed their every suspicion."

I put the bowl aside. "What happened?"

She smiled. "Kwesi and I had gone to the resthouse— to pick up some groceries—and the pickup died right in the middle of the market." Kwesi was a close friend of Melody's who worked at the institute's office. "Since Kwesi was driving the truck, naturally I got out to push."

I started to smile. I could see the scene Melody would have made. In the market, the women would be sitting in rows behind their stalls. Each would display to best advantage her one or two wares—she sold no more than she could carry the several miles to market. Heaps of charcoal. Basins of ground grains. Purple, brown, and white beans. Glossy black fish, smoked to a curl. Peanuts in red shells spilling beside wrinkled okra. Black polka-dotted guinea fowl tied in twig cages. Red earthen jars resting on their sides, their mouths o's of darkness. Each item represented hours of her labor—planting, watering, harvesting, sifting. Hours shown in the bulge of her biceps and the calluses on her hands.

The paths between stalls would be full of shoppers and playing children, and perhaps—on passes from the secondary school—some students wearing crisp ironed smocks and lipstick. Muslim traders dressed in brilliant calf-length robes, matching caps, and gold watches would be striding along to more important destinations, stopping briefly to greet one of the turbaned Muslim missionaries clasping a Koran. In the shade of the trees edging the market, men would be whiling away the hours playing checkers and *aware* as the bus drivers awaiting gasoline slept.

Into this scene of afternoon heat Melody would have descended from the truck, calmly moved to the back, and put her shoulder to the metal without thinking about what kind of sight they formed—a Ghanaian man in the driver's seat of a foreign car, a plump white woman with small hands pushing it.

Melody smiled at my smile. "I looked up," she said, "and there were just these rows of wide eyes. Everyone was staring. It's the only time I've been in the market when there was complete silence."

I shook my head with a grin. "So what happened?"

"Well, meanwhile, Kwesi's been trying to get the truck started, so he leans out the window and yells, 'Push!' And everyone looks at me in shock, like 'What's she going to do now?' and their eyes are like saucers. And I—well, you know me—I just opened my mouth and laughed. And the place shut down. I have never seen so many people laugh so hard in all my life. Two men had to hold each other up."

"Only you," I responded helplessly.

"I know, I know. My life. So then, of course, everyone comes over to help me push, but we're all pretty useless

148

because we're laughing so hard, which means the truck won't start, so everyone's giving advice but it still won't start, when who should appear on the scene but the inimitable Mr. Quarshie."

I sobered, remembering her opener about the police Jeep. "I don't understand. Why'd he arrest you? For blocking traffic?"

"He didn't arrest me," she said cheerfully. "He offered us a ride home."

"Oh."

"Kwesi and I hopped in the back—it was one of their paddy wagons—and the ride was worth the look on Dean's face when he saw us wave from behind the bars."

The greeting prevented me from voicing any thoughts. "*Ko-ko-ko.*"

I turned to the front door. The screen acted like a scrim, masking what appeared on the darkened side, but the adumbrated, lean frame could only be one person.

"Eh, Daniel!" I greeted, pushing off the table. "How is it?" He bent his head to enter and stood with awkward grace in the small kitchen. Long limbed and thin, Daniel came from a northern tribe. His face was angular and his eyes clear. He wore Western clothes: sandals, trousers, and a long-sleeved shirt open at the throat. Daniel attended the same bible study in which we had met Isaac and Stephen.

He grinned and gave a small nod. "It is well. How is it with you?"

"We are well," I responded.

A few weeks before, Daniel's fiancée had come from his village to see him, and he had brought her by to visit us. As it happened, my housemates were out of town, and I entertained the two alone.

Although I attempted conversation with Comfort Rachel—Western names she was no doubt unaccustomed to being addressed by in her village—we did not converse.

She told me her name and smiled at me but looked down, still smiling, when I asked anything further. Daniel answered my questions naturally, telling me where she came from, what she was studying, and how her journey had gone.

Daniel later gave me a photograph of her that surprised me. She was standing in a cornfield, her hand curled around a cornstalk, smiling impishly at someone who was not the photographer. Her large eyes made her seem young. "I wish I could have known her better," I told him, thinking of the many women I had met and missed.

Speaking with African rural women was always difficult. Perhaps Comfort misunderstood my English. Perhaps she did not comprehend me: the natural connections a woman might have with another—children, men, domesticity—were absent. Or perhaps she considered it polite to forgo the privilege of speaking to me. Whatever the case, my experience with her was common.

After my attempts at conversation with Comfort, I spoke to Daniel alone, listing my housemates and their activities. I felt Melody's absence keenly, sure that she would have coaxed Comfort into speech. Melody's ease with others often provided me a way into places I could not have gone on my own.

"So, when is the wedding to be?" I asked, smiling to include Comfort.

Daniel looked at his hands. "Well . . . ," he said, and shrugged.

Perplexed, I asked, "You have not set a date?"

He hesitated. "There is some small problem."

"What is this?"

He spread his hands. "Well, actually, we're not having the bridewealth."

"Oh, Daniel."

"These are hard times. What can we do?"

Comfort was no longer smiling.

"No one has been seeing cloth these three years," he explained. Cloth was often a major part of the bridewealth.

I was silent and then said, with a quick smile, "Just a moment." In my bedroom closet lay a piece of wax-print cloth I had bought in Lomé. At the time, I had had no good reason to buy it, but it cost only ten dollars. I thought I would find some use for it. I pulled its weight from the shelf and smoothed the pattern of white rings on deep blue. Perfect, I thought—twelve yards and an unobjectionable color.

I returned to the living room, smiling. But as I walked toward them—the only moving point in our triangle—the cloth got heavier and heavier in my hands. Daniel stared at it. It wasn't to be expected that even I, a rich American, would have such a commodity. His eyes did not lift from the cloth. By the time I reached him the cloth seemed heavy as gold.

I handed it to him, no longer sure what I carried. The words I had prepared in the bedroom seemed inappropriate now, but I said them as if he could give them back to me. "It would give me pleasure for you to have this." My smile had faded, and all three of us looked down at the cloth in his lap. Then I looked up.

He was weeping.

He struggled to speak. "We had despaired . . ."

Daniel came by more often after Comfort's visit, because, I think, he felt it proper considering the gift. And, as time went on, I was more at ease with him, the memory dimming of that moment when I knew my Westernness to be inescapable, as real as the sheltering gates of the American Embassy in Accra.

I shut the screen door after Daniel and turned to Melody. "It is the man with the beautiful fiancée!" I announced, teasing him.

"Well . . . ," he said, with a smile, "I am proud of her."

"Melody is just now making the meal," I told him, giving way to the dinner party that seemed to be forming. "You will stay?"

When we first came we had been unprepared for the visitors who arrived at mealtime. We pretended we would be eating later, so we wouldn't have too little to go around. Soon we were shamed by the many dinner invitations we had from our Ghanaian friends, for in their houses anyone who arrived at any time was fed. Copying them, we started to prepare stews and soups so there would always be enough if we added a little more rice.

"Thank you," Daniel responded and nodded.

Soon after we had seated ourselves in the living room with glasses of cold water, Isaac arrived. A strong breeze blew in the door as I opened it for him. Perhaps we really would have rain tonight.

We shook hands, snapping our fingers at the end. Isaac had a tribal scar along his left cheek and large teeth. His arms bulged from his short-sleeved shirt, and a fan of veins led from the inside of his elbow. The way he carried his muscled frame reminded me of a restless horse on a tight rein. He was accustomed to making larger movements than those required in a house. Seated, his foot vibrated on the floor.

After greeting Isaac, Melody left to check the stew. He leaned forward, as if he were debating following her, but then glanced at us and did not.

Isaac often came to discuss decisions with Melody. Their close relationship was unexpected, given his background. Isaac came from a powerful northern tribe, known for their warriors and rigid ideas about men and women.

Once, Melody and Isaac had argued all evening about the duties of husbands and wives, Isaac insisting that certain tasks, such as washing dishes or collecting water, were beneath a man with a wife and Melody insisting that love said otherwise. Later that evening, I entered the kitchen to fetch a glass of water. Isaac and Melody were sharing their thoughts about emotional healing while he dried the wet dishes she handed him. I was about to chuckle at this irony when they heard my step and turned as one, their faces echoing a smile so open and artless that the sound died in my throat. As I walked away, a comment Mary had made came to me; about how she had learned to accept from the way Ghanaians accepted her.

Melody had just called some question to Daniel when Stephen and another friend of ours, Frederick, knocked at the door. Isaac looked up as if he had been cheated. He had not expected all this company. I wondered what he had come to discuss.

Frederick entered the living room and shook hands with each of us jovially. He wore a striped shirt that matched his black trousers and the white curled slippers of a maharaja. Playing the dandy was a part of Frederick's genial nature. One day I had taken him to the back door to photograph him in the light there. He had shoved his hands into his pockets and laughed, and when I saw the picture months later his exuberance leapt off the print and startled me into a smile.

Frederick's humorous manner masked a purposefulness, however. He was self-educated, a stenographer, and a writer. He had had a short book published. It included a series of letters between a secondary school girl and an older friend. The girl had been seduced into a relationship with one of her teachers and was wondering what to do. The teacher had sent her gifts—a set of mathematical instruments and an English grammar book—objects whose allure tell the story of Africa. He offered no perfumes, no silks, only the hope of education. "I couldn't resist them," she wrote. "I have fallen into a vicious circle. . . . No, I don't think I love him. But my heart." The friend's replies were tender, and the advice frank. In the end, the girl broke off the relationship, returned the gifts, and told her friend, "The Lord has used you to deliver me from a web."

After greeting Melody in the kitchen, Stephen entered the living room. He was short, his face cherubic despite his mustache. He had the springy step of a pugilist. His shirt had cuffs and a collar, and he wore his fat tie loose but knotted.

I thanked him for the eggs, and he nodded without smiling, dismissing them.

We settled in a circle in the living room. Each face—slick with sweat—gleamed in the lantern's glow. Our bodies, dull with clothing, withered to shadows for lack of light, making our company appear disembodied, our expressions unusually animated.

Frederick raised the topic of the day. For weeks we had been wondering what the government's new budget would be. The head of state, Jerry Rawlings, had promised never to devalue the currency, but many outsiders had been recommending devaluation as the only way to attract foreign investors and revive the economy.

"I hear the new budget is out at last," Frederick commented. The others nodded. They had heard this, too. "J.J. devalued," he added.

Stephen gave a snort of disgust. "As for these khaki boys, what do they know about economics?" Stephen was not enamored of the military government of Jerry Rawlings, which had come to power a year and a half earlier. Rawlings's regime was merely the latest in a series of military governments, but Stephen, like most Ghanaians, still felt civilian rule was the only legitimate government for Ghana.

Rawlings had been a thirty-two-year-old flight lieutenant when he first seized power in 1979. He had gained fame before then for his messianic hatred of corruption and his swashbuckling flying style. Once in power, he promised a purging revolution. Ghana's previous coups had been bloodless; his first act had been to execute three former leaders—one of whom, General Acheampong, had amassed a personal fortune of $100 million at the country's expense. Rawlings's soldiers then destroyed the huge Makola market in Accra for being the center of *kalabule,* or black-market trading. Rawlings's youth, low rank, and mixed African-Western heritage made him a first for Ghana.

"Have you seen the budget?" I asked Stephen. Ghanaian politics fascinated me. The country was small enough for people to discuss politics as they would their family's affairs.

Stephen pulled his chair forward and his trousers up. I felt a sense of anticipation. Stephen always answered my political questions at length. The topic was too dear, and his sense of outrage too great, to allow brevity. Furthermore, the evening stretched ahead with no other prospect than conversation, as did the next evening, and the next. These friends often visited, and we had no reason to treat any topic summarily.

"Well," he stated, "a budget has been read, and the people have been asked to accept it. There is no discussion of it." Stephen operated on the firm conviction that others had fed me a "pack of lies" from which I needed to be weaned. As a result, he always spoke to me as if I were a reporter who had just interviewed his opponent—no fact was too basic to be introduced properly.

He shook his head. "If you have any adverse view on the budget you are branded as antirevolutionary, antipeople, reactionary—well, anything you can think of." After pausing to sip from his glass of water, he continued, his voice strengthened with contempt. "But I am telling you that we can say for sure that as of now Rawlings is being guarded heavily, but we, those in Ghana who are Christians, believe that the arm of flesh will fail you. We know for sure his day will come, and he's going by the same way he came. And we will not be wrong, neither disturbed nor disheartened, to say that he might die a foolish death. For he came by the foolish method, and he will go by the foolish method."

Isaac, Daniel, and Frederick exchanged glances.

"Some people like him, though, isn't it?" I prompted, hoping to hear their thoughts. While the four were in agreement that Rawlings had made mistakes, the opinions of the three other men were milder than Stephen's. They had some feeling, I think, that Rawlings was sincere and genuinely concerned with the plight of the people. Certainly many other Ghanaians felt this way. The three remained silent when Stephen talked politics, however, as people do when another feels strongly.

Instead of answering me, the three looked at Stephen.

He frowned. "The people really know the truth. They have a really good idea what the whole thing is about. They see that these guys are out to do nothing but cause rancor and bitterness in the country. In fact, many have lost their lives and many people are killed. People are asked to report 'with immediate effect.' " He scornfully mimicked the soldiers' attempts to sound educated. "That is the only language these boys know in their whole life. You report and you don't come back home."

"Who is asked to report?" I asked.

"Well," he responded, turning his mouth down, "anybody who is an enemy, whom the government labels an enemy. They don't mean an enemy according to the dictionary definition, but anybody they think is experienced, mature. Anybody who doesn't toe their line of thought. They brand such a person their enemy, and some are invited and never seen again. People are killed here and there." He indicated these places with a wave of his hand. "Many have died and many are still dying and many are going to die, because all over the nation Ghanaians have vowed to overthrow them whatever the cost." He nodded. "Their day is coming."

I shifted in my chair. "Stephen, you always talk of revolt. But don't you think Ghanaians are too peace loving to take up violence?"

He laughed, conceding to the pupil. "It is true, Ghanaians are by nature peace loving. We really want to live in peace, as anyone who comes from the outside will really realize, since we Ghanaians are living in a state that is next to slavery." He smiled mournfully. "The problem is that someone will want William Wilberforce to come on the scene and set the Ghanaians free."

We laughed at his allusion to the famous English abolitionist. I thought of the taxi driver who longed for the British, and of Rawlings—who was called "The Messiah" even in the press. The old days are always better, and we always long to be saved from ourselves.

Daniel took advantage of the pause. He sat on the far side of the living room, almost beyond the lantern's sphere of light. "Forgive me for saying," he challenged, "but it was the students who wanted Rawlings." Daniel was politely reminding Stephen that those who now protested most against Rawlings were the very people who had aided his rise to power—the students—of whom Stephen had been one. "We, the educated fools," Stephen called them.

"Well, I have been a student," Stephen acknowledged, pulling out his handkerchief and blowing his nose resolutely. He folded the handkerchief and arched his body to push it into his pocket. "And I think I am still a student, and I hope to continue to be a student for some time. People are accusing us that when Rawlings came we supported him." He shook his head with force. "No, we didn't! When they came, they came on the thirty-first of December, 1981, and everyone who is conversant with the educational calendar year will tell you that the students were on holiday when this disappointed European and his crew of cohorts came on the air."

"Wa!" Frederick exclaimed. "The students did noth-

157

ing for this revolution?" Frederick's arms were akimbo on the armrests.

Stephen responded indirectly. "I think that we students in general owe a service to the country. We are always wishing to see the lot of the Ghanaian peasant improved," he asserted and looked at Frederick. "At every stage of their so-called revolution, we try to evaluate them, and, being very much abreast of the facts, we are convinced that they need to hand over." He nodded. "As the bible says, a soldier man is not trained to rule. Anyone who has been abreast of the news in Ghana since the time of Acheampong will agree with me: as long as the students say he will go, he will go. Whether he likes it or no, he will go."

"Why will he go?" I asked.

Stephen tugged his ear. "For the past few years we have had a series of military governments coming in to overthrow the popularly elected civilian governments, giving reasons of the civilian governments being incompetent, corrupt, inefficient, and what have you. And they promising us to do better than what the civilian government had done and the whole thing turning out to be that they are worse than the civilian government, if not hopeless. I mean, they are more or less helping us to accept the adage that the devil you know is better than the angel you don't know."

He paused, and, when he began again, his voice was no longer public but personal. He spoke earnestly to me. "You know, when 1981 was coming to its end, all of us were just looking up with fresh hopes to what the Lord might have for us in the years ahead." After two years, it looked like the civilian government would retain power. "Then," Stephen faltered, "the afternoon of the first of January, we, as usual, heard another unusual voice on the air—someone who was not the newsreader or the head of state."

Stephen came to a halt, deadlocked by the waters of

158

passion and despair. How many ways the dreams of a people are betrayed. And how amazing that they dream at all. The intensity of his love for this country was foreign to me, citizen of a country so distantly run.

Stephen began again, authoritative once more. "This voice was somebody who had come in by the help of external powers, especially Libya, to overthrow the popularly elected government of Dr. Limann. This voice claims," he scoffed, "that he has come to set the people free and make them a part of the decision-making process and a whole *range* of rubbish."

The voice belonged to Rawlings.

"It's peculiar though," I mused. "Rawlings was the one who made it possible for Dr. Limann to come to power in the first place."

In 1979, only three months after he had overthrown the military leader Akuffo, Rawlings surprisingly handed power over to an elected civilian government headed by the academic Dr. Limann. Two years later, however, on the New Year's Eve that Stephen spoke of, a disenchanted Rawlings staged another coup. Dr. Limann had brought "nothing but repression," he claimed. Since then, Rawlings had retained power.

Stephen spoke with disgust. "Yes, but Rawlings made the whole world to understand that the civilian government was on probation and if they don't do well he's going to come back. And people knew that, as usual, this was very childish talk and they just ignored it. You can be sure immediately Rawlings handed over he was planning to find ways and means to overthrow the government. Then, when he took over the second time, he said if the people of the nation do not agree to what he's done they could put him to the firing squad."

Stephen spread his hands and spoke like a prosecutor to a wavering jury. "But the question was, who at that time was bold enough or had the resources at his or her disposal to take him to a firing squad?"

159

We laughed. None of us could imagine Stephen with a gun in his hand. Despite his rhetoric, Stephen was not hatching any plots. He was a philosopher, not a revolutionary. Stephen did not smile.

"So, that was how the whole thing happened," he pronounced, leaning back in his chair. "He claimed he had initiated a revolution, and we were on a path to having back the smiles on our faces. But it seems as of now that we are having tears—and not mere tears, but we are weeping blood."

"Why?" I asked.

"Because. Our hospitals, which he claimed were graves when he took over, are now cemeteries. Our roads, which he claimed were gravel pits, are now stone quarries. Our economy, which he claimed was sick, is now dead. Our stores are more empty than ever, unemployment is on the ascendancy, and our factories have all ground to a halt. In the midst of plenty, we are living in total poverty."

There was a bleak silence. "What can be done?"

"We are hoping that someday we shall get the leadership of people who are matured and experienced," he replied harshly, "people who have families, who are not young boys like the regional secretaries who have not even completed their university education. And therefore, they have not even had the chance of waking up in the morning with a baby crying, trying to figure out what is wrong with the baby, let alone coming to lead a whole nation like Ghana. These rogues will talk to their fathers' coequals as if they were their juniors at school." He sighed. "We have a lot of bright guys, and yet we are leaving the nation to be led by a lot of crooks and people who don't know their left from their right. The people of Ghana thought they had a good dream because they knew Rawlings to be an honest guy. But he has proved hopeless, and the earlier he goes, the better it stands for him. The bible says that any step of the fool is a step further to aggravate his foolishness, and this is exactly what we find with the government of Chairman Rawlings."

I only then noticed Melody standing behind me, waiting to announce dinner. Stephen's language—rich and rhythmic—had carried me beyond the grim political realities and out of the bare room. Beauty and terror intermingled in each of his sentences, his voice coming to me like a lifeline unlooping over still water.

Melody brought out clay bowls of rice, corned beef stew, and boiled eggs, whose perfect ovals glistened against the rough pottery. In the pause that falls just before eating, I looked at each familiar face around the table—Stephen lifting the lid to the stew, Isaac and Daniel finding room for their legs, Melody examining the table for any lack, Frederick flipping open his napkin—and I realized, suddenly, surprisingly, that I longed for no others.

"Isaac," Melody said, taking his hand and mine as we all followed suit. "Will you say grace?"

Isaac nodded, ducking his shoulders.

"Lord God, Father," he prayed, "you are the owner of this day. You are the one who is known but never fully known. You are the king who cannot be found out by searching." He hesitated, his head lifting slightly. "Pass over our sins. Amen."

We ate using knives and forks, though we didn't always. Our plates rested on the bare wood, nicked from use, and a single kerosene lantern glowed at one end of the table.

When the first hunger had passed, I returned briefly to Stephen's comments. The question of violence was something I had been considering since the arrest.

"Ghana's different from other places," I told Stephen. "There *is* trouble here, but not rampant violence or chaos. The political violence is nothing like what happens in Uganda or Beirut. When the former leaders were executed here or those judges murdered, people were shocked.

Not just because it was horrible, but because it was unusual. It had never happened before. Look at how people reacted when they merely arrested William Ofori Atta." Mr. Ofori Atta was a folk hero whose wisdom and quiet courage had made him popular since before independence.

Stephen nodded. "The news spread like a bushfire in the harmattan. People were very annoyed with the government. They had to let Pa Willie go. In fact," he added, "when he was arrested under Acheampong, that was the straw that broke the government's back. Everyone was against the government."

"You see?" I said. "Ghana is different. Once, Mohammed was in the market and two men started yelling at each other. People gathered, thinking they would see a fight. The men were on the verge of blows when a spectator shrugged and turned away. 'As for these men,' he announced, 'they think we want to see them hit each other. What do we care? They shame themselves.' "

Daniel and Frederick applauded my accent while I continued. "Everyone stared and then someone started to laugh, and then everyone was laughing. The two men shook hands and walked away. And do you know what Mohammed said to me?"

Stephen raised his eyebrows.

"He said, 'That is the way we are. We take things seriously, but we do not care to fight.' " There was an acknowledging laugh around the table. "You see what I'm saying? Other places are not like that. They will fight over things they don't even take seriously. I'm telling you. Something is different here."

Stephen shrugged, uninterested. "I don't know about those places," he commented, "I'm only knowing this place. And I am asking"—his voice was bitter—"how much longer must we bear this? Even the Ghanaians who have been kicked out of Nigeria are all trying to return there. They say they would rather die in Nigeria than suffer in Ghana."

"Hmm," Daniel said, giving a sad chuckle. The others shook their heads. I gazed into Stephen's eyes and then shook my head, too. Who knew when it would end? I was not the only one feeling trapped.

We ate for a while without speaking. The solitary call of a bird sounded long and mysterious as the wind furled the tree branches against each other. The flame in the lantern was steady, our faces unwavering.

Melody rested a wrist on the back of her chair and spoke to Isaac. "Did you visit the Harts today?"

Isaac nodded and frowned. The Harts were missionaries with the conservative church Isaac attended, the same church Pastor had served. When I was a child, our family had attended the branch of their church in Accra two or three times: my brother and I liked it because they distributed American bubble gum in Sunday school.

"How did it go?"

Isaac grasped his fork with a fist and pulled the tines through his pursed lips. "I don't know whether you know her," he replied, as if he had been waiting to talk about this. "She served us fifty-eight minutes of standing on the outside of the house. In all this time, she is not inviting us into the house or given us a drink of water. And she is even outside and went inside without reason." He extended a hand in appeal, his fingers curled and paler on the palm. I saw him on that porch, only a step from either the African soil, or the cool Western interior, and yet a lifetime away from both.

"That is *too* bad," Daniel said with a frown.

"For fifty-eight minutes."

"Hmm," Melody sympathized.

Isaac pushed his empty plate forward and crossed his arms on the table. "Here is what is happening," he said. "We were asking for Mr. Hart, the husband, to fetch us some of these tin sheets for making the roof of the new

163

church. Either getting them from Togo or maybe getting them from Upper Volta."

"What did he say?" Frederick asked, laying his fork down.

"It so happened, he agreed."

"Really?" Melody asked, surprised. Isaac must have shared his doubts before going.

"Well," he confessed, "he said he would, but he didn't want to give too much hope. I told him, 'I am a Ghanaian. All I have is hope.'" Melody shook her head.

Stephen was puzzled. "I thought Trueblood was getting the sheets for that church."

"Well, in fact, I'm hearing about this thing, that he collected the money." The men all glanced at each other and then away. Frederick clucked his tongue.

"What are you saying?" Melody asked, watching them. There was a silence. "That he raised the money but hasn't bought them?"

Isaac lifted his eyebrows and shrugged.

"Isaac," Melody said, shocked. "He can't do that!"

"Who's to say no?" Isaac responded with acerbity. "It is part and parcel of this man! He who could have sold his car to a brother, but who instead just sold it on *kalabule* for the highest price."

"I remember that," Melody acknowledged. Isaac had been very angry about the incident.

"You can't even see how Trueblood has helped the local church," Isaac continued. "Rather he has made her his instrument. It is such that if you are not involved it will even be hard to tell what is happening." He frowned at his plate. "Anyway," he added, "I'm only hearing this. I don't know. Perhaps he will yet buy them. I'm only knowing that these people are not interested in national endeavors. Except for Hart."

Isaac had explained the group's lack of interest to Melody and me before. This American-based church had separate black and white administrations. The Ameri-

164

cans, all white, took care of the American missionaries, and the Ghanaians took care of the Ghanaians. The money raised in America for the church was used strictly for the white missionaries. "They won't send guys to the U.S. to learn," Isaac explained. "They don't encourage their people to send money to us for buildings or trucks."

Confusion about this issue reigned until the annual all-church meeting one year. People were gingerly approaching the topic of money and its allocation, when one of the white missionaries stood and said, "Look. I'm going to explain it to you all like it is. Our people send us money, it's for us. Your people send you money, it's for you. We're not interested in spending our money on your projects. The funds from the U.S. are for our houses and our cars and our children. For us. Not you."

Isaac's reaction to this statement astonished me. I would have been incensed. The whites had access to the kind of money the Ghanaians didn't. For the whites to withhold it from the joint work of the gospel seemed a crime.

But Isaac's primary emotion was not anger. He was glad, he told us, that at last someone was being honest and clear. As a Ghanaian, Isaac understood the higher call of tribe. "We can see the way that it is. We can accept it, that the money from their people should be for them." He said the Ghanaians at the meeting were disappointed but felt they had found something valuable, a man they could count on to be forthright.

The first thing the church did was to recall the man to the United States to reprimand him. It was still unclear whether they would allow him to return.

"Good," I had said with relief. "They thought twice when they heard the truth stated so baldly."

Isaac snorted. "Rather, they chastised him for revealing their secret." He watched for my response.

"You're kidding."

"I'm not kidding," he insisted.

165

"How could they do that?" I asked.

Isaac shook his head. To him the recall was the most senseless action of all. Just when it seemed a door had been opened, it was forcibly shut.

Melody remembered something. "So why did Mr. Hart agree to buy the sheets? I mean, if they're not interested in your projects?"

"Mr. Hart, maybe, I would say, is not the same as these others. In fact, that is why they want to remove him," Isaac added grimly.

"Him, too?" she asked with surprise.

"In that like manner. Trueblood will stay, and Hart will go."

Startled by his anger, Melody queried him. "I thought you didn't like Hart?"

"He's an OK guy. His wife, well . . ." His expression was speaking. "She controls the affairs of the house. She won't be enjoyed. She has a problem feeling fine about helping us. It looked like he knew her character and wasn't obedient to his parents." Isaac looked at Melody knowingly, implying that Hart had married his wife against advice. "One time even, he sent her instead of himself to speak to the church elders. That time we were really insulted."

Given the church's extremely conservative policy on women, Isaac was correct to construe their behavior as an insult. Hart's wife would never have been asked to speak to a group of white men. On the other hand, perhaps Hart was more liberal in his interpretation of a woman's role than his church. If so, it would be typical of the cross-cultural miasma that what made Isaac the angriest would be, to me, their saving grace.

Even if we had not heard Isaac's opinions, we would not have admired the Harts. Unlike the foreign translators, the Harts made no concessions to their African surroundings. A private generator, run on expensive gasoline, insured their home of twenty-four-hour air-conditioning. Rust-colored carpet ran wall to wall. Overstuffed, dark furniture filled their rooms. The VCR and TV were set in an elaborate console, the wood cracked from arid air and the latticed speakers encrusted with insect trails. Among the plastic knickknacks and murky landscapes hung their one acknowledgment of the locale: a crude African oil painting they had bought in an airport. Every Christmas for their annual card, Mrs. Hart wrote a poem stiff with rhyme and iambic pentameter, declaring their "burden of carrying light to the heathen."

For all their parochialism, however, I agreed with Isaac that the Harts were not in Trueblood's category. I had had only one conversation with Trueblood, at a get-together of the expatriate community at their house. We met while I was watching their TV and sipping a Coca-Cola—both unaccustomed activities. The show had been taped from American television, and the sound was off. A woman bounced in silence across the screen, her hair floating behind her. She pulled out the bottled magic that transformed her hair to slow motion, and the image resolved into an unshaven man lifting a pistol.

Trueblood launched into a monologue on the natives. His tie and belt were tight, the rest of his clothing loose, his stance professorial. "The Ghanaians have to learn to stand on their own two feet," he declared. "Like we did. Until they learn to be independent, they'll never be anything. They're always here asking for stuff. Gimme, gimme, gimme."

I shivered in the air-conditioning. Don't answer a fool, lest you become like him. But also: Answer a fool, lest he think himself wise. Which one?

I remembered a family trip to Lomé when I was twelve. At a stoplight, a beggar advanced on our car and shoved his hand through my father's window. The man

167

was tall and muscular, but—I saw over my father's shoulder—his fingers were cruelly twisted. They made a mockery of his strong back.

"I beg you. Dash me small for chop," the beggar insisted.

My father's profile came into view as he eyed the beggar. "No dash," he said, "but I am a doctor."

The beggar began to snatch his hand back, but my father was quicker and caught him by the wrist. He turned the beggar's hand in the light from the window. "Today you have been lucky," my father said. "Watch."

And one by one he pried the beggar's fingers loose from where they had been tucked behind each other. With a flourish, he released the beggar's hand. "You are healed," he pronounced.

Menace crossed the beggar's face. The wall of the building behind him glowed like a red sea. Then he let loose a bellow of a laugh. "Eh," he exclaimed, "you have really worked a miracle, man!"

"It was nothing," my father responded, smiling. "For you, no charge." The beggar laughed again, pushed his hand in to shake my father's, and moved down the row of cars. As he strode away, he was already folding his fingers back, his large frame bent to the task.

Fumbling for words, I asked Trueblood who had gotten Africans addicted to Western things. He switched sides.

"And what better way than the American way has ever been invented?" he asked. "Everyone depends on the U.S. If the U.S. went under everyone would go under. America is beautiful because it gives people what they want."

So why did he blame people for wanting it?

"I don't," he said, contradicting himself. "I just want them to recognize that the West has provided everything of value in the world."

He didn't consider Christianity valuable? When he

stared at me, I reminded him that Christianity had started in the Middle East, that it was an Eastern religion, not a Western.

"Well, it may have started there, but the West spread it, the West made it what it is today."

"What it is today," I repeated, thinking of Ireland and the Ku Klux Klan and then, on another tack, the Ghanaian Independence Day speech I had heard recently. "The missionaries came," the regional secretary had bellowed across Tamale's military parade ground, "and told us to lay up treasures in heaven. Then the traders came and aided this process by taking all our earthly riches. Truly, I say to you, seek ye first the political kingdom!"

What could I possibly say that would change this man's views? I felt paralyzed and wished that I could disavow myself of everything he claimed—being American, white, and Christian. On the TV, a speedboat trailing a smooth wake exploded.

Encouraged by my silence, Trueblood was making larger and larger statements. Cross-cultural sensitivity was ridiculous, Ghana's only hope was the West, Ghanaians were lazy.

"Why do you bother?" I interrupted. He straightened, sensing in my tone something out of sync with our friendly conversation. "You despise everything around you. Why are you here?"

He spoke with cold dignity. "I'm here to sell the gospel."

For a moment I was stunned. "Tell me," I said at last, "is the price still thirty pieces?"

Remembering that conversation, I looked across the table at Isaac. He was tracing a grid on his plate. On an impulse I said, "I really admire you."

He looked away from me, embarrassed, and then back. "Why?"

"For getting past them." I laid my fork down. "If I

had to deal with them I don't think I would be a believer."
When Isaac shook his head, I insisted, "No, I mean it. I
don't think I would be."

Isaac dismissed this. "They are missionaries," he said.
The offhand comment struck me as loving: their faults
so easily swept away! "They are not the church. You can't
confuse them."

"It's a tribute to you, Isaac, that you see it that way,"
I said. "I don't know how you forgive them."

He looked down. "They have a saying here, 'It is
because of the dog's master that they are patient with
the dog.' "

I smiled. "That's lovely."

Isaac rolled his glass of water between his two rough
hands. "I will tell you something," he continued. "I know
the name of Christ to be true. No mouth can soil it. We
give the devil a chance to say how big he is when we
panic at these people."

I nodded, grasping the comfort he offered. "Well, Isaac,
I salute you." I touched my forehead with my fingertips
and he smiled. "There is also a saying, isn't it?" I asked,
looking to Daniel for confirmation. "People are like your
fingers; some are taller than others."

Daniel nodded, pleased that I knew the proverb, and
at Isaac's frown we released all our darknesses with
laughter.

Frederick pushed his chair back, sensing the conversation's change in tone. "I know a funny story about these
your friends, Isaac."

We smiled at his adjective: Frederick's stories were
always funny. Isaac hooked his arm around the back of
his chair, and Daniel leaned forward to adjust the flickering wick of the lantern.

"Yesterday, in the market," Frederick said, "I met
the cook for the Truebloods. He don't look so cheerful.

This is what he tells me." Frederick eyed each of us to engage our attention. His voice took on the storyteller's fullness.

"Mr. Trueblood is always calling his wife by names other than her name." He nodded at Daniel's puzzled look. The others had apparently heard of this practice. "Instead of her Christian name he will use some word. One of these names he is always using is"—his voice vibrated with supressed delight—"honey."

"Honey?" Daniel asked, tickled. In some of the northern parts of Ghana a man would never use his wife's given name, much less call her a food.

"Honey," Frederick emphasized. "And," he added, leaning forward, "most of the time he is only saying 'hon.'"

Both Melody and I laughed at Frederick's pronunciation of our own favorite. His mimicry of an American accent was pure caricature, the *o* round and prolonged.

"Hon," the rest imitated at the same moment, which made us laugh all the harder. The rolled *o* belonged to a drunken Santa Claus.

Frederick continued. "The cook is coming from the bush. He doesn't know these people's way. So one day he is coming into the dining room and he says to the wife"—he struggled to keep his face straight—"he says: 'I be needing money for market, hon.'" The men roared with laughter. "He thought it was her name!"

Frederick shot up, and put his hands on his hips. "And Mr. Trueblood says, very angry"—Frederick mimicked—"'She's not your hon, she's my hon!'"

Stephen almost fell backward out of his chair. Daniel and Isaac laughed with open mouths. We had to wipe the tears from our eyes.

"Oh my," Melody gasped.

"These Americans!" Isaac added. Frederick waved a stern finger at us, still holding the angry expression, and then collapsed with a triumphant grin. And every time

171

we thought we had stopped laughing, the image of the cook's consternation and Trueblood's indignation rose before us afresh.

We adjourned to the living room then, sitting down in a close circle, with our legs outstretched and feet interlaced. A moth fluttered around the lantern's glow. Air stirred through the back door, open on the African night. The static of insects blanketed us. For a time we were silent, enjoying the breeze, sipping our water, and knowing our friends around us.

Frederick began telling riddles. He didn't often do this, as African riddles were difficult for us to guess, but that night they seemed appropriate: at once strange and true.

"My father built me a house," Frederick started. "It has no windows or doors. What is it?"

We puzzled over this riddle, but couldn't name what object fit the description.

Frederick supplied the answer, "An egg," and gave another riddle. "When my father and mother gave birth to me, I was one. Then I gave birth to many and they go everywhere with me."

"These are too hard," Melody protested.

"The hairs."

"What?"

"When you are born, you are one person. Then you grow hair." Melody groaned. Frederick continued, "My mother and father brought me forth the first day. The next day we die, the next day we are there and so on."

Stephen spoke up. "The sun, moon, and stars."

"Very good," Frederick replied. "Last one. My mother and father brought me forth in a big lake and there is only one fish."

Daniel smiled. "I know that one. It is the tongue."

Stephen, sitting opposite from Melody, nodded at her. "I have a riddle you will know."

"Yeah?"

"Out of the eater, something to eat. Out of the strong, something sweet."

"That's Samson's riddle!"

"The answer?"

Melody creased her brow in thought, then shook her head. "I know the story. Samson finds a lion's carcass and inside it a bees' hive. He tells the riddle at his wedding feast. I just can't remember the exact answer."

"It's simple," Stephen said. "What is sweeter than honey? What is stronger than a lion?"

"There is perhaps another answer," Isaac added. "What is sweeter than life? What is stronger than death?"

"Out of death, life," I agreed slowly, seeing rotting ribs embracing the swarm. From that sight, other images rose. A cross flowering in the desert. A bush that burns but remains green. Water lying still as in the womb. The Africans say the snared bird sings sweetest.

I heard Isaac say he should be leaving. The wind was gathering and whipping the trees. Our neighbors were outside collecting their possessions and setting them on their veranda. The husband shoved a water barrel under a rainspout from their roof as someone inside clinked their louvered windows shut.

"It won't rain on you?" Daniel asked Isaac, looking doubtfully at Isaac's thin shirt.

"No, it wouldn't."

Nevertheless, Daniel went and picked up the umbrella he had brought. "I will come with you that way." Isaac nodded.

Isaac paused in the doorway as Daniel held the screen door open. "You guys have been quite lovely," Isaac said, his hands braced against the frame.

"Be careful," Daniel warned, placing a hand on Isaac's shoulder and looking back at Stephen and Frederick. "Or curfew go catch you," he added, using the pidgin English phrase. Stephen nodded. Frederick, after looking at his watch, stood and left with Isaac and Daniel. The curfew imposed by the military was approaching, and he had a distance to walk.

Stephen had to leave soon, too, but the three of us sat down again for a moment. The conversation turned to our departure from Ghana, which, Stephen mentioned, was fast approaching since Easter was already upon us.

"Not so soon," I demurred. "Over a month away."

"The time will pass quickly," he responded.

"Yeah." At the thought of leaving, the companionship of the evening began wearing off like wine. Would I leave Ghana no closer to a solution? The room seemed barer without the other three.

"By the way," Melody said, turning to me, "Kwesi says the fares will go up with the new budget. Flying from Tamale to Accra will cost a small fortune."

"Really?" I frowned. "How much?"

"You could live for a month on the money."

I sighed. "Where am I going to get that?"

She shook her head. "I don't know."

We were tired, it was late, and we fell into the kind of conversation we would have avoided usually. We grumbled about the high cost of living, bemoaned the poverty of our accounts, and protested the lack of alternate transportation.

Stephen spoke. "How many cedis will the ticket cost?"

A warning bell rang faintly, but before I could speak, Melody had named a figure. "I guess," she added. "Why?"

He stood up decisively. "I will bring it tomorrow." He shook his trousers straight.

Melody laughed. "Oh, Stephen."

"Stephen, really." I kept my voice light, unconcerned. "Don't do that. We're just complaining. It'll work out fine."

"I will bring it tomorrow," he repeated. My mouth dried. I knew the look in his eye. What had we been saying? How could we have been so stupid as to mention a need in front of him?

174

"Don't be ridiculous, Stephen," Melody said sharply. He looked at her.

"Stephen!" She raised a distracted hand. "You know how I exaggerate. It's nothing." She saw his face. "Well, not nothing. But I wasn't thinking," she pleaded. "I haven't the sense I was born with."

"You are needy. I will help you," he stated.

Melody started to speak, but instead began to cry. Stephen sat down. He did not touch her.

"You are needy. I can help you," he repeated, as if speaking to a small child.

"Stephen, that's ridiculous. We're filthy rich compared to you." The words tumbled out, a truth never voiced about the chasm between us.

He spoke once again. "I can help you."

She began to laugh through her tears. "You are absolutely the most obstinate man I have ever met! I don't know why I put up with you."

"Tomorrow, then," he said, insisting.

"Tomorrow, then," she repeated, her shoulders slumping.

He stood and spoke to me. "I will come by tomorrow morning."

I stood, too, and crossed the living room to him, hoping to gain time. How could I persuade him to lay this idea aside? Such a costly gift was more of a burden than I could carry.

Then I was in front of him, looking into his still eyes, and it all fell away: the day, the heat, the stark room, even Joseph's glance as he exited the tin shed. Eye to eye with Stephen it came to me. Just accept. It's like grace.

Like honey from the lion.

I extended a hand: Stephen didn't like emotional sloppiness. "Thank you," I said simply. Stephen beamed like a candidate and wrung my hand. Pausing at the front door, he gazed through the opaque screen as if he might say something, and then he was gone.

I returned to Melody. She let the hand over her eyes fall and stared at me.

"We don't deserve it," she said.

"No, we don't," I agreed, feeling an absurd joy. "C'mon. I'll wash, you dry."

We went out to the kitchen but halted when we saw the stacks of dishes. We would have to boil water for a long time to finish them. A crack of thunder reported through the house.

Melody looked at me. "Let's go outside, onto the veranda," she said. "Leave this mess."

Outside, the trees were rustling, sounding like surf. A gust of cool, damp air swooshed past. Lightning marbled the sky and froze the trees in midtoss. The first drops came, pocking the dust, testing the dry earth's readiness. A moment of anticipation, and then rain collapsed out of the sky, breaking like a dam.

"C'mon," Melody shouted to me, pulling me by the hand. "C'mon!" she shrieked as the first drops hit her, and suddenly I was running.

My sandals were off, the dust already turning to mud under my toes. The rain pounded on my head and sluiced down my body. It drenched the posts of the house and the lintel of the door, and the concrete absorbing water turned dark like blood.

It seemed as if the earth was giving birth, the lightning blooming like yellow flowers in the sky, the air smelling sharp as onions—just as, oh once so long ago, it had smelled in Ethiopia. I had only to open my mouth to turn water into wine. My hands and feet and tongue were flapping like sails as I scudded over the mud, inebriated by the wind and water: whirling, laughing, and shouting "Alleluia!"

PENTECOST

The Coming From

The flame trees surrounding our bungalow had ignited into flower. Their blooms rose like tongues of fire among the yellow garlands of new leaves. Bees hummed from bush to bush as birds trilled scales. The grass was translucent with light, the sky blue as an eye. Every object appeared haloed.

The rains had brought the land to life. One morning we had woken to find our dust lawn covered with tiny blades of grass. We would not have been more surprised to see it strewn with emeralds. "It's like waking in the Garden of Eden wearing rags," Melody said.

I breathed the morning in: the cool air smelled rusty with fecundity. The sound of someone washing told me our neighbors were rising. Lowering my packed suitcase to the veranda, I pushed aside a plastic bag and several yams, and settled between them on the top step.

Beyond the flame trees lay a road, and beyond the road a field, recently hoed. A flock of black birds darted across its rows. A woman balancing a basin of water did not turn aside for a passing motorcycle: no dust rose behind it. The grass growing at the road's edge feathered in a light breeze.

I leaned forward to embrace my knees, hoping to hold the moment still. Over the last few days, events had begun speeding up, as if pushing me to gain escape velocity. Later, I would look back and see those days as shot with a flash: parts bright with sharp detail, the rest forever receding into darkness.

But for this moment, I insisted on slowing down. I plucked out the book that poked from the plastic bag. Six hundred miles from Accra, on a trip north to stay with translators, I had found on their bookshelf, quite by accident, a dusty children's book about Scotland, inside of which was scrawled, in my own childish hand, "Wendy."

I opened the book, resting it on my sandaled toes, and flipped through the mildewed pages. Though the drawings had begun to seem familiar, my signature remained strange. How labored the letters looked, as if writing had absorbed my entire being. Now I could not even remember what year I had penned it, my name like a scar whose cause has been forgotten.

I flipped back to the beginning and once again followed the story. Wee Gillis spent half the year in the highlands and half in the lowlands. The highlands taught him to hold his breath while stalking deer, and the lowlands taught him to bellow the cows home. One day he stumbled across a bagpipe so large no one could play it. He picked the pipe up, drew in a deep breath, and blew the huge bag full. The deep, clear note sounded across the plains and over the mountains. The plot was one I remembered from childhood. I wondered if the ending had seemed real to me then.

Birds rose in startled flight from the field beyond the road. Two Ghanaian men walking along the road toward me had disturbed them. I closed the book, pushed it into the plastic bag, and stood. Were the men coming to visit me? I looked at my watch. I had to visit the director's house and the office before leaving.

The week before, I had finally written the newsletter account of my trip to visit Mary. I had been avoiding it with singular devotion. Although none of the pieces I had written for the newsletter had been easy—the bright, chatty tone the newsletter required not being my forte—the article about Mary had stumped me for months. My uncertainties about her ran too deep. Galvanized by the thought of my departure, however, I had written an account of Mary's life that, once written, seemed appropriate. It concentrated on the more colorful parts of her daily life, and carefully outlined her heroic qualities. If not brilliant, it committed no egregious sins. I had presented it to Mary uneasily, but, to my relief, she had read the piece and suggested only minor changes. When I dropped the article off on the director's desk, my tasks here would be complete.

Descending the veranda steps, I recognized the pair turning off the road into our yard as Pastor Abraham and an elder from the church we attended. The pastor was a dignified man in his fifties. He wore a goatee and glasses with thick black frames. The cane he carried signified status, not weakness. The man accompanying him was younger, thinner, with an intense gaze. He assisted Pastor Abraham every Sunday by translating the sermon.

I halted, smiling. Their visit was an honor seldom accorded, and a pleasure, given Pastor Abraham's remarkable character. While in his thirties, Pastor Abraham had decided to learn to read and write. Having accomplished this, he enrolled in a four-year college to train as a pastor. Now he was the pastor of one of the main churches in Tamale.

This midlife change had been no easy movement. Besides the expected difficulties of switching from farming to academics, his nephew had tried to poison him.

Pastor Abraham's pursuit of a foreign god brought shame to the family. But such events did not stop Pastor Abraham, who claimed to have eaten the poisoned stew and walked away unharmed. It was too vital, he told the congregation, for Africans to become pastors. Africans could spread the gospel better than foreigners. "You can't tell if *oburoni* is leading a life of deception," he had said, "but if he is one of your own, his life is open."

Pastor Abraham's language drew me. His sermons were a mesh of the biblical and the African, full of folk wisdom and color. On Palm Sunday, he focused on the palm tree, showing how its virtues mirrored Christ's. Another Sunday, he gave a comic minidrama, acting out a wife and husband arguing through their children. The skit's images and insights, though draped in humor, were precise.

In midsermon he had once shouted, "You don't want money, you want heaven!" At the rustle in the pews, he lowered his voice. "As for that," he acknowledged, "we want money." He gave a wry smile at the general laughter. "But we don't love it so much that it will lead us into trouble!" he thundered, back on track.

Pastor Abraham usually preached in English. His translator, the young man visiting with him today, tried to follow in the local language, Dagbani. Pastor Abraham started off slowly enough—completing only a sentence and then waiting until the translator had finished translating—but soon he was racing along at breakneck speed, spitting out whole paragraphs before pausing only long enough to catch his breath.

His impassioned voice rode a range of decibels and paces, but the translator's was always the same, a steady gallop. Each phrase came out clipped, since he often had to listen and speak simultaneously. He was a gifted translator. At some point during every sermon, however, he would get lost, stumble, and give up in exasperation. Pastor Abraham would stop to offer apologies, someone would

182

make a joke, and the pair would be off and running again.

Hearing a sermon in translation can be tedious. But with Pastor Abraham and his translator, the pauses—which made repetition a necessity and subtlety a danger—provided time to meditate, and the interaction of the two men offered enough material to fill any gaps.

The morning of their visit, Pastor Abraham and the translator stopped below me on the veranda steps, and the translator greeted me for them.

"I am well," I responded. "How do you find the morning?"

"It is well," he replied.

"And your wife?"

"She is well."

"And your children?"

"They are well."

"And your farm?"

"It is well."

I gestured toward the door. "You are welcome," I said, and they followed me in. When seated, the translator told me the reason for Pastor Abraham's visit.

"We are hearing that you are leaving this day."

I nodded. "This is true."

The translator pointed his chin toward the older man. Pastor Abraham sat, shoulders back, with both feet planted on the floor. His gaze did not flicker from my face. "Pastor Abraham is hoping to give you some words of encouragement before you return to your homeland."

I folded my hands, uncertain what would follow.

Pastor Abraham spoke to me then, in English, beginning with a quote from the bible, Isaiah 55:1, which states, "Ho, every one who thirsts, come to the waters." *Ho* is a word commonly used in Ghana, and at first I thought Pastor Abraham was paraphrasing the quotation. Later, when I looked the reference up, I saw for myself that it led the verse—bold as a shout.

Where Pastor Abraham came from, he told me, there

were "big woods." When Pastor Abraham called someone by his name in these woods, "he wouldn't hear me." The woods were too thick, the sound overcome. "No, if I want to be reaching him, I call *ho*." Only the pure, single note would a person hear.

Isaiah started this verse with *Ho,* Pastor Abraham continued, because the people he spoke to were at a distance. They had wandered away too far to hear. Pastor Abraham paused then, making sure I understood this point before he went on.

"Christ is God's *Ho,*" he explained, as his speech began to flow. "He is a sound so pure, he is a sound so righteous, he is a sound so powerful we can hear him even in the big woods where we are lost, far from God, woods so big we are not hearing our own names. That is why God sent us his own name. Because we could not hear anything else. This name we hear calling us to him, calling us out of the big woods, calling us to the deep waters. There we will hear our names, and we will know our names, and we will lie down and we will drink and we will never be thirsty again.

"In the place where you are going, there may be big woods. There may be many voices. There may be much confusion. But you must always be listening. Listen for God's *Ho*. For in the beginning was the Word, and the Word was with God, and the Word was God. And neither is that word beyond the sea, but it is very near you, it is in your mouth and in your heart."

We sat without stirring. Throughout this speech his eyes did not leave mine, and I did not break our gaze when it ended. I felt rooted, anchored in stillness. Then Pastor Abraham nodded and settled back, his mission accomplished.

Conversation lagged, but neither guest seemed restless, so I did not grow anxious. After a time, Pastor Abraham nodded slightly to the translator, who announced that it was time they left. As we stood, I shook the translator's hand and complimented him on the translating job he did every Sunday.

His face became more somber. "Since the beginning, Christianity is depending on translation," he said. "It is a privilege to confound the Tower of Babel."

I nodded, and we moved out onto the veranda.

The three yams stacked by my suitcase caught my attention. Food was still scarce in the urban areas, so I was taking some supplies with me for my week in Accra. Pastor Abraham scanned the field beyond the road while the translator wished me a safe trip. I, without thinking, bent to pick the yams up. The words were out before I considered what response I might get.

"I hope you will take this small thing," I said, handing the yams to Pastor Abraham. I paused—remembering the incident with Daniel—and my last words came more slowly. "I am grateful to you, for your preaching of the gospel this year, and your words of encouragement today." I switched my weight to the other foot. What would he say?

The translator beamed as a mother does when her child unexpectedly demonstrates good manners. Pastor Abraham nodded gravely, as if a gift were right, to be expected. And I nodded back, hoping through imitation to gain some of his dignity.

I watched the pair walk away, the translator measuring his gait to Pastor Abraham's, until they were hidden by the flame trees.

Inside the director's house, I placed both hands behind me to prevent the screen door from slamming shut. Bent next to the ham radio was Mary. The radio broadcast only static: her contact hadn't come on yet. Writing engrossed her; only her ear peeped from her gray hair.

I crossed the room. "Hello."

She looked up abruptly.

No chair stood next to her, so I leaned against the

radio table, my hands gripping the edge. "Dean told me you would be here," I said. "I'm leaving soon, and I wanted to say good-bye."

Mary nodded.

"Thanks for your help with the article," I added.

Her nod was slow in coming.

Growing uncertain, I glanced down at the radio. "Who are you hoping to talk to?"

"Accra."

"If I can help by taking anything down, I'd be happy to."

She shook her head. We were silent.

I looked at my watch. "I should be getting back to the house. Kwesi's coming by in a few minutes to take me to the airport. I just wanted to say"—I pushed my hands down my skirt—"good-bye, you know, and . . . thank you."

Her gaze did not meet mine.

"I'll never forget . . ." The words tumbling in my mind never reached my lips. Our curtain was descending.

She interrupted me. "I want to ask you something."

"Anything."

"Don't . . . Don't print the article."

I stared at her. "Why?"

Her words were simple. "It's a schoolgirl's view. It would embarrass me."

I was speechless. I looked up and away, and somehow my tongue moved. "All right."

Watching me, she opened her mouth as if to speak, and then moved as if she meant to rise, but in the end did neither. I must have said something else, but I don't remember that or leaving.

Back at our bungalow, I wandered aimlessly through the rooms. A clanking in the hallway was followed by a chugging sound. The water had come on. I fetched the short hose and hooked it up, placing the opposite end in the water barrel. I stared at the water whirling in the bottom. It would be full in several hours. I was putting a note on the dining room table—"I left the water running"—when I heard Kwesi's truck pull up.

At the airport, two Muslim women prayed, the fluidity of their bowing suggesting fervorlessness. They sat like deers, their heads twisted over their folded legs. A girl leaned back against her grandfather, the back of a hand over her mouth, and stared at me.

Heading down across the country toward the coast, we flew low enough to see the circles on circles of villages. The sun shone on the brown waters of the Volta like palm oil on groundnut soup. As we left the plains of the north behind, the land altered from brown to green to limitless blue.

The time in Accra I spent idly, at loose ends. The day before I was to leave, I walked down to the beach. Near the city, the beach was full of debris—worn plastic, sodden fabrics, and tangled, rotting plants. I picked my way among them to a clear space and sank to the sand. The sun glinted off the water beyond the breakers.

I thought of Mary. I remembered Carol mentioning Mary's disappointment when I could not visit her that first time. I thought of the article and knew it for what it was: a reduction that made Mary appear both smaller and larger than life, its cheerfulness relentless even in the face of mystery. I thought of all my errors—the lost chances, the hidden prejudices, the unspoken thoughts. And now this article. And thinking of it, I put my head down on my hands as if some wound there would be cauterized by the salt of tears.

The next night, I walked out into the warm darkness. The plane loomed over me—smooth, monstrous. Light seeped from the tiny windows high above. Its squatting hulk was a self-contained world, separate from everything here, from the black moths that always covered the inside walls of the airport after the rains. The stale, metallic breath of the airplane repelled me, but I ascended the steps, into its maw. Inside I was surrounded by synthetic objects and suddenly claustrophobic, I turned to smell the ocean one last time, but the door was falling into place, and it was gone.

Once in Amsterdam, I stood waiting in line for my transfer ticket. After months of venerating Western efficiency, the irony was not lost on me. People walked by in the chill of the airport: odorless, noiseless, colorless. The lights glared on floors that seemed painfully antiseptic.

For three days I flew to reach Seattle. I did not sleep. The hour before we landed in New York I gave up on a letter and rubbed my eyes. Before me the writing turned to black and white patches, a grid whose pattern reminded me of a kente.

Then, as we started the descent to Kennedy International Airport, I saw against the far side of the 747 an impossible sight. A black moth, just like the moths in the airport in Accra. I don't know how it came to be on that flight or how it was possible. I had transferred more than once since Accra. But there it was, across the airtight ship, bumping from light to light to light and flying on. In the womb of this ship, a black seed and I, waiting to be born.